C000126548

The Mariner

TALEB ALREFAI

The Mariner

Translated from the Arabic
by Russell Harris

Banipal Books

The Mariner
First published in English translation
by Banipal Books, London 2020

English translation copyright © Russell Harris, 2019

First published in Arabic 2004
Original title: *Al-Najdi* النجدي
published by Manshurat Thatalsalasil, Kuwait, 2017
© Taleb Alrefai 2017

The moral right of Tayeb Alrefai to be identified as the author of
this work and of Russell Harris to be identified as the translator
of this work have been asserted in accordance with the
Copyright, Designs and Patents Act, 1988.

No part of this book may be reproduced in any form or by any
means without the prior written permission of the publisher

Cover photograph by Alan Villiers
© National Maritime Museum, Greenwich, London

A CIP record for this book is available in the British Library
ISBN 978-1-913043-08-7
E-book: ISBN: 978-1-913043-09-4

Banipal Books
1 Gough Square, LONDON EC4A 3DE, UK
www.banipal.co.uk/banipalbooks/

Banipal Books is an imprint of Banipal Publishing
Typeset in Bembo

To Abd al-Aziz al-Dakheil
A lifelong friend and brother

The walled city of Kuwait does not appear at its best, seen from the anchorage, but it has one of the most interesting waterfronts in the world. There are more than two miles of it, and the place is one great shipyard of Arab dhows. All along the waterfront, running east and west along the shore of the shallow bay . . . the big ships and the little ships jostle one another.

Alan Villiers
Sons of Sindbad (London, 1940)

This novel is a fictional retelling of what might well have happened to Captain Ali Nasser Al-Najdi, and is based on real events that took place on Monday 19 February 1979.

Chapter 1

11:30 a.m.

"Come."

I was perhaps five years old, I remember, the first time I heard the call of the sea. I was a child sitting on the front stoop of our old home in the Sharq neighbourhood, where a narrow dirt path separated our family home from the coast. I never stopped hoping I'd see the dhows lying on their sides on the sandy shore, and behind them the sea. A strange question would whisper inside my heart: What had the sea done with the big ships to make them so small on its distant lap?

The sea went on calling me:

"*Come.*"

Wearily, the sun sank down to sleep in the depths of the sea, as the sky spread the ashes of darkness across our house's outer walls and inside our rooms. My sister Maryam sat in the courtyard, busily wiping soot from the glass lanterns. She'd wind a rag around her small hand and push it inside the glass mouth to clean the insides. Beside her sat my mother Fatima, who seemed distracted, yet was closely watching the movements of my sister's hands. I left them to go to my sister Latifa back in the kitchen, as I loved to eat flatbread hot from her hands. She would peel a loaf from the metal griddle, then wave it in the air to cool before handing it to me. She noticed me and said with a smile:

"Come back in a bit, and I'll have your bread."

I told no one about how the sea called to me. I evaded my mother and sisters and slipped out of the house.

When darkness heard the voice of the muezzin calling the evening prayer, it descended from the sky. Because men were afraid to face the dark, they stopped work and hurried off to the mosque for prostrations and prayers. The path in front of our house was empty of passers-by, except for a few boys running to the mosque.

I was not afraid of the dark. In a moment, I'd crossed the dirt road, and my bare feet sank into the sand. Here, I heard the call of the sea more clearly:

"*Come.*"

I sat on the damp sand and looked into the distance, to where the sea meets the sky. How many times I'd wished I could walk upon the sea! I'd imagined I could walk all the way out, between the sea and sky. My head would be in the clouds while my feet were on the water. I stretched out on the wet sand. I don't know how the breeze came over me, nor how the darkness closed my eyes. "Ali. Ali."

The repeated calls snatched the covers off my slumber, and I became aware of the cold damp sand against my ribs.

"Ali."

I opened my eyes in the darkness. The roar of the waves quickened and filled my ears, chasing away my drowsiness.

"Ali!" I recognized the sound of my father calling me.

"Yes."

I saw two ghostly shapes fighting their way through the darkness: my father carrying a lantern and, at his side, my oldest brother Ibrahim.

"God forgive you," Ibrahim said. "We've been looking for you for the past hour."

They came nearer, and I stood and took refuge in the folds of my father's dishdasha. He handed the lantern to Ibrahim and lifted me to his chest, kissing me. "My son."

In that moment, I was afraid. I felt I'd made a mistake.

"What if our neighbours, the Fadala children, hadn't seen you heading down to the sea?" Ibrahim asked.

"Don't ever do this again," my father told me, adding: "The sea could take you, and then you'd drown."

"I wouldn't drown."

My father stopped, as did Ibrahim, who was holding

4

up the lantern. I looked into my father's face.

"The sea's my friend," I told him.

Behind me, a wave echoed with words I didn't understand.

"The sea doesn't have friends," my father said, with a note of pain in his voice.

I held back the question: *Why doesn't the sea have friends?*

★ ★ ★

Now, memories come flooding back to me. On that day, I was five years old. More than sixty-five years have passed since that night. Rest in peace, Father. I wish you'd lived to see how your son befriended the sea, and how the sea offered him friendship and gave him life in all its abundance. But Father, the secret call of the sea still fascinates me. Fate decreed that your son be born a mariner whose sights were set only on the sea.

Father, in your hands I became a sailor and a captain – a *nakhoda*. I first sailed the sea on your boat, at your side, with you as the captain. I too became one when still a young man, and so the sailors and the people of Kuwait came to call me "Nakhoda".

Father, I am the shark that dies the moment it leaves the sea. Since I left it, life has abandoned me. The loneliness and desolation of dry land have not stopped gnawing at my soul ever since I embraced the sea. It calls to me, and I go to it, as if hypnotized. I have lived my life in its vast house. Many times, it was cruel to me, but it has never forsaken me.

Father, did you ever imagine such a friendship between the sea and a man? Between the sea and a drop? I am that drop in the heart of the sea.

I set aside *Sons of Sindbad,* written by my friend, the Australian captain Alan Villiers. The book tells of his travels with me on my dhow, the *Bayan*. For the last two days, I have been leafing through its pages. I read bits of it and look at the pictures: ones he took of me and the sailors, of sections of the dhow, and of the seaports.

It was more than ten years ago that a friend gave it to me: "Published by the Arab Book House in Beirut".

I long for these memories of my time at sea, and I return to the book. I leaf through its pages, and with it, the stages of my life. I re-live its most beautiful moments. The trip I can never forget.

I sit down with my wife. "Noura," I say. She turns toward me.

"Listen to what Captain Alan says about your husband the first time we met, in the office of the merchant Ali Abdellatif al-Hamd in Aden."

I read to her: "He was a small, slight man . . ."

"You aren't small," Noura interrupted.

"Alan was tall, so he thought I was short. Listen to what else he has to say: "with a strong face . . .""

"Your face isn't strong."

I smiled at her and went on reading: "He was handsome, in his own way, with an oval face, a close-clipped black moustache, a hawk nose, and a well-defined, determined chin. He was wiry and lean, and he looked strong . . ."

"Well that's true," Noura said with a laugh.

"Just listen. Listen! 'There was about his face and all of him an air of strength and goodness, and of alert ability which augured well for any ship he might command, and of complete self-assurance which boded ill for any who tried to thwart him . . .'"

"That sounds right." Noura cheerfully interrupted. I looked at her. A deceptive calm fell between us.

And before me the sea.

Yesterday, when we were having our nightly get-together in my *diwaniya*, I came to an agreement with Abd al-Wahab and Sulayman:

"Tomorrow, we'll go fishing."

This was not the first time. We scarcely went more than a week without a fishing trip together.

"I'll be at your place before the noon prayer," Abd al-Wahab had said.

"You're welcome, I'll be waiting for you two."

"Noura," I call to her, so she'll look up from where she's sitting. "Abd al-Wahab and his brother Sulayman are coming over here."

This statement surprises her. She realises I'm planning to go out to sea.

"The sea," she says, her voice tensing with affectionate reproach. "The sea has bewitched you!"

That happened a long time ago. It has been a lifelong love affair.

A cloud moves across her face. "Stay with me today."

Her request is strange. She adds, in a pleading tone, "Don't go."

My heart is touched by something hidden in her tone. I wish I could do as she asks, but I say: "We've already arranged it."

"Make an excuse. Say the weather's too cold."

"I can't. The two of them are on their way by now, and they might be here any moment."

"It's no use, it's your nature. Your words never change, and you never back down."

"A man's worth is in his word, Noura."

I notice her staring at my face.

"We agreed on this yesterday."

She stays silent, but her restless gaze says everything. I smile and urge her: "Say it."

"I'm afraid for you. May God prolong your life, you're over seventy."

"The sea brings youth back to my soul."

"May God keep you safe," she says resignedly, then asks: "When will you be back?"

I hadn't yet given that a thought, nor come to any agreement with Abd al-Wahab or Sulayman.

"I don't know."

She keeps looking at me, waiting for a clarification.

"We'll be back by evening."

"Your attachment to the sea makes me anxious."

"The sea's my second home."

What I don't tell her is that the sea is calling to me. I remember what I'd said many times to my friend Captain Abdallah al-Qutami: *My end will be in the sea.* I pity Noura, and don't tell her about this.

It's as if I can hear the sea calling out to me, "*Come.*"

"Do you want me to make something to take with you?" Noura asks.

"There's no need, I already arranged it with Abd al-Wahab and Sulayman . . . I'd better get changed before they arrive."

"Don't be late coming home."

"I'll try."

I stand up, holding the book. Noura follows me with her eyes. I smile at her and say: "Listen. Let me read you what Alan Villiers wrote about the Kuwaiti sailors once he'd got to know them, and then you might forgive their love of the sea."

I flip through the book's pages. "Listen: 'I had grown to like the Arabs, especially this . . . group of Sindbads who dwelt on our poop. Sindbad himself if he ever existed . . . could not have concocted adventures such as were commonplace with them."

Noura looks at me, and I add: "Alan was talking about the Kuwaitis when he gave his book its title."

"I know, Abu Husayn. You've told me that already."

I give her a farewell smile: "I'll go and get changed."

★ ★ ★

Noura had set aside a special section in the wardrobe for my clean seafaring clothes. A few days ago, my eldest grandson Nasser told me: "One of al-Rabah's sons says hello." I looked at him, and he added: "He sees you when you visit the shop of Ahmad al-Rabah, his grandfather."

I tried to call the shop and the boy's appearance to mind. Smiling, Nasser added: "He's impressed by your style. He told me 'Your grandfather always has such clean and neatly ironed clothes and cloak, which smell of incense and agarwood oil.'"

"Your friend flatters me."

Nasser laughed. "No, Grandpa, everyone knows how much care you put into looking smart."

He said nothing for a few seconds and then added: "My friend says they can smell you coming."

★ ★ ★

I put on my heavy sea-going dishdasha and place a kufiyah on my head. I walk up to Noura and give her a farewell look.

"May God keep you safe."

"We'll be in God's hands."

I go out and stand by the door.

My house is in the Kayfan neighbourhood, which is beside Shamiya. The only sounds are those of the passing cars. The small dirt road still separates my house from the sea, which I can no longer see when I open the door. The damp smell of the sea washes over me, reviving me, and it stays with me as I walk.

The air is cold. It's February. *You're old now, Ali. You have to take the cold into account.*

★ ★ ★

Two days earlier, when I began leafing through Alan's book, the pictures had rekindled my love of the sea. My boat came back to me, with me sitting in my special spot, or standing beside the tiller. My thoughts flashed back to the mast, the sails, the crew, the songs, and the harbours. I remembered the words of Yusuf al-Shirazi, that kind sailor who was in my service: "You're the most important mast on the boat, Captain."

The days of my youth come back to me: how I'd sailed with my friend Captain Abdallah al-Qutami from one port to another, from one country to another, to buy and to sell. How we built good relationships and gave friendly gifts to the elders and notables of the tribes all down the cost of Southern Arabia. Abdallah used to say to me:

"Such extravagance."

I would smile back at him and say:

"That's how the business is won."

He would keep looking at me, and I would add:

"Generosity is good for humanity."

The photographs in the book stirred my memories of the days that had been dimming in my heart. I saw many faces without knowing from whence they'd come. I could see myself hoisting the mainsail in the headwind, which then filled out the mizzen sail to the accompaniment of the sailors' voices chanting:

> *"O God, O God*
> *We entrust ourselves to You*
> *God, keep us safe!"*

Those memories had become part of my very being.

I was seven when I finished memorising the 'Amma' and 'Tabarak' sections of the Qur'an. I had studied for a year with the mullah, who was a friend of my father. Every morning, I would go to his house with the children from the lane. We would sit on the rush mats as he stood before us with his long stick, his red-hennaed beard, and his booming voice. He taught us reading, writing, and the basics of arithmetic. I remember the day he told me:

"You learn quickly. You'll be the imam of a mosque someday, God willing."

"I'm going to be a sea captain," I said.

"Better an imam than a sea captain." He silenced me, irritation entering his tone. I did not understand the reason for his anger.

"My father is a sea captain, and I'm going to be like him," I said again.

He raised his voice to scold me: "Quiet. Don't talk back." He pointed to the pole to which our legs would be tied when he wanted to beat us on our feet:

"That's what happens to children who can't hold their tongue."

I hated how he shouted at me and was angered by his threat. I imagined myself lying on my back, two boys holding up my feet, which would be tied to the bastinado with a rope, and I pictured him striking my feet with his long stick. I could not bear to sit in front of him. After a while, I stood quietly and left the other children, the rush mats, and the hot shack.

"Sit," he shouted at me.

I ignored him, and his voice rose: "Sit down, boy!"

A boy got up to grab me, but I kicked him before he could lay a hand on me. I left the mullah behind me with his sessions, the children, his long stick, and his bastinado while, barefoot, I went home. I told my father:

"Your friend the mullah shouted at me and threatened me with bastinado. I'm not going back tomorrow."

"What happened?"

My father told me to finish my lessons with the mullah: "After the mullah, you'll go to the Mubarakiyya School."

"But I'm not going to go to the mullah or to the Mubarakiyya."

He looked at me as if he were waiting on my decision, testing my resolve.

I said: "I've learned how to read and write, and I'm going to sea."

★ ★ ★

Sulayman's car is coming. It's closer . . . It stops, and Abd al-Wahab climbs out.

Sulayman's voice greets me from inside the car: "Good morning to you, Captain!"

The word thrills me, and I answer:

"Good morning to you."

"Are you ready?" I ask Abd al-Wahab.

"We've bought all the supplies."

"Get in," Abd al-Wahab calls to me.

He always insists that I sit in front, beside his brother

Sulayman, who does the driving.

He says: "Since you are the Captain and the pillar of Kayfan, you sit in front."

The trip from the Kayfan neighbourhood to the Mariners' Club, where the boats are moored, takes less than half an hour.

"It's cold today," Sulayman informs me.

"The sea will be warm," I tell him.

"Only if there are fish to be had," Abd al-Wahab asks, jokingly. "As you remember, last time . . ."

"Be optimistic."

"God is generous."

I sit beside Sulayman as he steers the car towards the harbour.

Chapter 2

12:30 pm.

The sea is clear today. A cold breeze plays with the surface of the waves.

When we arrive at the al-Shaab Mariners' Club, we're met by the place's particular smell, and we carry our supplies from the car to the boat. I check the vessel's two engines and the petrol in the stern before heading to the bridge.

The warmth of the sun fills the glassed-in wheelhouse. Abd al-Wahab and Sulayman get busy putting away the supplies.

Sometimes I wonder about my yearning to meet the sea, I ask myself: How long I will be able to keep doing this? It's as if my soul is only at ease when I am on a boat's deck, rocked by the waves.

Lately, the sea has been making its secret call again: "*Come.*"

"Ali!" Abd al-Wahab calls out to me, pointing to the cassette player and tapes. I smile and ask him:

"The Awad al-Dokhy?

"The one and only Awad – and Shady al-Khaleej!"

The sea is calm and smooth, the February sun warming its surface.

"You can't go sailing without music," Sulayman says.

"We ready to head out?"

"That decision lies with the captain," Abd al-Wahab says, adding, "We trust you."

I turn the wheel and feel the boat's hull rise. The club's jetty is utterly calm, and I can see no movement.

"To the Aryaq fishing grounds?" I ask Sulayman.

"Definitely," he says. "But it's cold, so I hope we won't be late getting back."

"Your brother's worried today." I address Abd al-Wahab, adding: "You'll decide when we turn back."

"When the captain is here, no one else can make that decision."

"We won't come back late," I tell Sulayman to calm his worries.

We always go out fishing together. Almost every week . . . The smooth sea helps us make good time, and the powerboat happily streaks away . . . We head south in the direction of the coast of Saudi Arabia, leaving a white line of foam behind us that trails away as we sail on.

Whenever I head out on a sea trip, my heart beats as if I'm making my maiden voyage. I am again that young boy who cried with longing for the sea.

When I was thirteen, I told my father:

"We've made a small boat."

He had just returned from his evening prayers, and we were sitting together on the ground. He was about to have his usual evening meal – small loaves of flatbread baked by my mother or my sister Latifa, which we dipped in a bowl of yoghurt, and dates. He looked at me with the beginnings of a smile, and I continued:

"Me and my friend Muhammad al-Qutami."

"Did any of the boat-builders help you?"

"Your friend Hasan the boat-builder gave us lots of help."

He was well aware of Hasan's skill and craftsmanship in working with wood, and his voice brightened: "God bless you all."

This encouraged me to make another confession: "We've been taking the boat out every day for the last two weeks."

"I know – Hasan told me. And I saw you a few times, too."

I got up and kissed him on the head, hoping he would take me with him on a pearl fishing trip.

"All the boys in Kuwait go out to sea," I said. "Staying at home is for women."

A contented smile brightened his face: "God willing."

I understood what he meant and flew with joy, running off to tell my mother the good news. But her face shrank with a sudden fear.

"No, son. You're still too young."

Her voice was hoarse as she held back tears: "I will not let Nasser take you out to sea."

I hugged her, then kissed her hand and head.

"Oh God, please! All the boys in the neighbourhood . . ."

I reminded her that two years earlier, I'd helped the men working on the wall around Kuwait City, and that, even though we were exhausted from fasting during the month of Ramadan, back then she'd encouraged me to go with my brother Ibrahim: "You are a man. Off you go with them."

"Walls are one thing," my mother said, refusing. "But going out to sea is another."

I don't know how it happened, but tears came against my will. I pressed on: "I'm not a kid anymore."

"But you're crying like one!"

I realised I was crying over the sea, and I wiped my tears with the edge of my sleeve. "I won't cry."

"Nasser! I made you swear by God you wouldn't take Ali out to sea with you." My mother, may she rest in peace, had made my father promise not to take me pearl diving with him that summer, and he gave in and went back on his decision.

Awad al-Dokhy's voice drifts into the pilot's cabin:

Were I to spill my heart to the starry sky
Stars would fall straight down, by and by

Sulayman busies himself with a crate of fishing gear, happily sorting out the lines, hooks, lead weights, and bait. Abd al-Wahab as usual has taken out *al-Qabas* newspaper, and he fiddles with the cassette recorder before he comes over to ask me:

"Do you like the singing?"

I turn to him. "You know I do."

He keeps looking at me, and I add:

"Before any trip, I'd search for the best singers to take with me on the dhow. My father would say: 'When souls are happy, they sing.' And I would answer: 'When souls sing, they're happy.' I could never set out to sea without a famous singer, one who had a beautiful voice, with an oud and a good drummer to keep up the beat. I would tell al-Mujammadi, the chief mate: "Just find the best singer and don't worry about the cost."

Sulayman comes over to us, and I finish the story:

"I organised a singing party in every port I visited – a big party with all the ships' captains, the tribal elders, the traders, the senior harbour officials, and the sailors."

"Everyone knows that," Abd al-Wahab interrupted, adding: "You are great-hearted, Ali."

"Generosity among friends is the stuff of life."

"The sailors still praise your generosity and the way you treated them, even though they've long given up going to sea," Sulayman says. "They still remember those musical evenings."

"Singing's a great help to the sailor. More than half the year, a sailor's away from his family and country, living through darkness and terror. It's easy for them to get bored and despondent. All they had to entertain them and keep their spirits up was God's mercy and music."

"Those days are long gone, Ali." Abd al-Wahab shakes his head while Sulayman stands there, listening.

"Now, the moment I hear any sort of sea shanty, I feel a ripple of life in my heart. I remember the mud houses on our lane, and the games boys and girls played in the dust. I hear familiar voices, and they bring back the coast, the sight of hundreds of boats at their moorings, the banging and clanging of the boat-builders as they sawed their planks, and as the 'gnomes' hammered them together to make sailing craft. That was the Kuwait of the twenties, thirties and forties. It was all sea, pearl hunting, and voyages."

"It was a hard life," Sulayman interjects.

"True, but it was a simple life with good and decent people." What I don't tell him is that, in all that hardship and poverty, I lived the best days of my life.

> *Down my cheeks, the tears slide*
> *Oh, I look back at my life*

The sound of Awad al-Dokhy's voice fills the bridge as he sings the words from Hamad al-Asousi's *Zuhayriyat.*

I haven't seen another boat since we left the harbour. Our boat speeds on, as if trying to outdistance itself. The sound of the engine breaks through the silence of the sea, and the boat creates a fleeting white line of waves in its wake.

Abd al-Wahab gets up and goes back to his newspaper.

"Abu Fayruz sends you his best wishes," Sulayman tells me.

I turn toward him, and he continues: "I met him at the market, and he told me to pass on his thanks to the captain."

I nod without saying anything, so he goes off to check the fishing equipment.

Last week, I visited Abu Fayruz at his home. I've made a habit of providing my mariners with a little help, and just being with them gladdens my heart. I can't give up my men, even if time has come between us.

Now, all that's left to me of the sea is these brief fishing trips ... Lately, I've started waking up with the roar of the sea around me. Just as it did in our home in the Sharq district, the call keeps finding me: "*Come.*"

I love the way the powerboat cleaves the sea's calm waters. I forget myself when I'm at the helm, happily steering its course and listening to the song of the sea.

"There's going to be some good fishing today." Abd al-Wahab makes this prediction from his seat.

"God is generous."

"How long is it until we reach the Aryaq?"

"Same as always, an hour and a half."

He goes back to his newspaper, and I to my steering.

I've never been good at driving a car. My grandson Nasser takes me wherever I want to go, and I enjoy his company and his stories. Once, he asked me: "What do you have against driving, Grandpa?"

The question hung in the air between us, and he went on: "Is it because you want to be a captain and steer a ship?"

I said nothing for a while. Then I asked him: "How can you compare a great ship with a small car made of tin?"

Yesterday evening, I left the house, taking the driver and going to walk in the old lane where our house had once stood. There was nothing left. The monstrous city had swallowed everything: the houses, the paths, the beach, the ships and the sailors' singing. I continued dragging my feet along until I stopped at Nuq'at Shemlan and looked out at the sea. I felt grief . . . and I addressed it: "You have become strange to me, dear sea, as I have become strange to you."

I went back home with the sea shouting back at me: "*Don't forsake me.*"

Next time I'll go alone – just me and the sea. Sulayman complains: "It's cold out here."

I don't want to be a burden on anyone. I'll go just for the pleasure of being together, so my soul will grow calmer. I'm past seventy now, yet I'm still that boy who's obsessed with his longing for the sea.

Nothing limits the view before me. The sea spreads out all around us, flat and sparkling with its welcoming waves. Whenever I go on about the sea in front of Nasser, he says: "If you wrote poetry, all your odes would be about the sea."

"Every lover writes about his beloved."

The sea is my beloved. The day my father refused to let me go because of my mother's wish, I stayed on my own, keeping out of her way. I spent my time with my friend Muhammad al-Qutami and our little boat. We were just discovering the secrets and delights of the sea, and we would stay by the sea all day long. My mother kept on trying to buy my affection, and I felt a little sorry for her. I scolded: "If you hadn't interfered, I'd be out there with my father."

"My son, you're still too young for the terrors of the sea."

"The sea's my friend."

"You're naïve, child, and you don't know anything about the sea."

That irritated me. A month had passed since the pearl diving season started, and I'd come to an agreement with Muhammad. I told her: "Me and Muhammad al-Qutami are going off to work at sea."

Her gaze tensed, but I went on: "We're going to work with a captain, selling water to the pearl fishing ships."

"You're not going." The threat was palpable: "I'll be angry with you."

Because I loved my mother and was afraid of upsetting her, tears burned in my chest, but I managed to control myself and walked away.

The sea is calm. The wind is no more than the hint of a cold breeze. The boat glides along, disturbing the sea's slumber, leaving in its wake the roar of the engine and a line of white foam. The words of the singer Shadi al-Khaleej reverberate through me as he sings:

"As you wander round the houses"

I turn to Sulayman. He's busy with the fishing lines, and Abd al-Wahab is reading the newspaper.

I hold on to the steering wheel and scarcely look at the compass. The route to the Aryaq is engraved in my brain. I don't need a compass to direct me along Kuwait's shores. Since childhood it's been my habit to commit the patterns and depths of the waters to memory the first time I make any sea voyage. I've sailed my ship the *Bayan* to the coasts of Africa and India . . . In comparison, the trip in this boat is just a quick jaunt.

I was perhaps fourteen years old the day my father gave me the good news: "You're coming out with us this season." I sprang up and kissed him on the head. Finally, I'd be joining my father on his ship for my first pearl fishing trip. I'd be able to follow the call of my friend, the sea. I'd leave the land far behind and be out at sea for months. I'd be sleeping on the deck, as close as I could get to the sea, and I'd live like a sailor.

The next morning, he took me with him. A captain was walking along the shore from the Sharq district to Qibla, getting the sailors ready and making sure the ships were fully prepared. The moment the first shimmering of summer could be felt, preparations for the pearl fishing season began. The whole shore would buzz with life and activity, and the sailors would all meet up, full of enthusiastic hopes for a good season, singing as they prepared the boats. The boats were hauled ashore onto dry land, but they'd soon be ready as the men thronged all over them, with full-throated singing of shanties and ballads.

I was thrilled to be able to share in their work. I helped to paint our ship with an oil extracted from sharks and sardines. I could hardly bear its strong smell, but I faced the task and finished it. With my bare hands, I stirred sheep fat and powdered gypsum together to make the paste that we painted onto all the lower parts of the dhow to keep her watertight and protect her from the salt water. It was my father who made the decision. He confirmed with the head sailor: "We set sail tomorrow morning."

That night, I scarcely tasted sleep, tossing and turning on my mattress on the floor, waiting to hear the dawn call to prayer. On the morning of the big day, after breakfast, I grabbed my bundle and eagerly set off for the water's edge. My mother kissed me. I remember her loving look, and I could hear the emotion in her voice:

"You're in a hurry to get to sea, my son."

She had her arms around me, and I didn't know how I could explain it to her. I would've liked to tell her that I hadn't slept an hour that night, as I'd been listening to the rumble of the waves calling out to me, again and again: "*Come.*"

"You'll be gone four months. Hunger and misery and . . ." She swallowed a word that had glittered at the tip of her tongue, then added "exhaustion".

"I know."

"I pray to God to give me patience while you're away, and that He will bring you all back safe and sound."

She was praying aloud for me, for my father, and for my brother Ibrahim. We were all going to set off for the pearl fishing season, and no one had any idea who would return. Tears were running down her face. She kissed me, and I slipped out of her arms. The moment I was outside the door, I ran off towards the shore, drawn by the secret call: "*Come.*"

I go and stand at the wheel so the glass cabin will protect me from the wind. The powerboat speeds through the waves as the motor throws up spray behind us. Only the empty vastness stretches out in front of us. I can't help imagining, as I often do, 'What if I could walk on water . . .'

The day I waded into the water alongside my father and climbed onto the dhow, my heart almost burst from my chest. This was my first pearl fishing season . . . It was the day of the *dashsha*, or 'the big off', and the shore was buzzing with activity as the people of Kuwait took their leave, crying as they shared prayers and dreams for the safe return of sons, husbands and relatives and hoping for a bountiful pearl fishing season. The sailors were given warnings about the unknown and of the dangers of pearl fishing, and perhaps even intimations of death in those summer months. The moment my father settled himself into the helmsman's seat by the rudder, he called out to the men: "The sailors' prayer."

As if the mariners had been waiting for this magic expression, they all responded:

"Fellow believers, give prayer and greetings to the Prophet of God:
O God, be with us.
O gracious God, O beneficent and merciful God."

The lilt of the prayer still rings in my ears:

"O God, we put our trust in You as we set out to sea.
I put my trust in you, O God,
My fate is with Your might,
You know the darkness of night."

I don't know why these memories come rushing back to me. Sometimes, I feel the sea is calling out to me to revive our shared memories in my heart.

It's as if the boat knows the route to the Aryaq fishing grounds, as if the sea is welcoming me.

Abd al-Wahab and Sulayman are paying no attention.

Every man understands and enjoys the sea in his own way.

On the first trip I made with my father, he admonished me firmly: "Keep your heart and ears open to every word I say."

While I was young, I took in my father's warnings: "Nothing is certain at sea. It can deceive you. At all times, keep your wits about you." His eyes took in my face as he added: "The captain always keeps the boat's position at sea in his head and heart: he notes every dip and swell, every breath of the wind, and every outline of the coast."

I still remember the details of that trip with my father as if it had taken place yesterday. First, we headed towards the fishing grounds of Shu'ayba, but my father then instructed the helmsman to head towards Umm al-Hayman. On the first night, the divers all took a laxative. My father leaned towards me and explained: "They need to have empty stomachs so they can fill their chests with a larger amount of air."

We lingered there for two days: "These spots are close to Kuwait, and the water is shallow."

It was my father who gave me my first lesson of the sea. He told me: "This is just a trial dive for the men."

Then we sailed for three days until my father chose the right spot for pearl diving, which we called the *hayr*. "God willing, it'll be a good spot," my father told me.

I tried to engrave in my mind and heart every word he uttered, as well as those from his assistant, from the chief among the seamen, and from the helmsman.

The sea is calm today. The sun is brilliant. The boat ploughs its way through the sea, leaving a white trail in her wake. Abd al-Wahab, as usual, is pouring over the pages of his newspaper, reading every last article and enjoying the music as Sulayman sits next to the crate of fishing tackle, entertaining himself by preparing the fishing lines. I'm behind the wheel, drawing my energy from the calm surface of the sea.

On a pearl fishing trip, the sailors wake up in time for their dawn prayers. They steel themselves with one date and a sip of coffee. My father told me: "The divers mustn't eat. They have to keep their bodies light so they can hold their breath for as long as possible underwater and collect the oysters."

A few days into our journey, I began to understand what my mother had meant when she talked about suffering at sea. The divers would start work at sunrise. Each would hold on to a rope attached to a heavy weight, and they would work closely with their diving partners, who would stand on board, holding the other end of the rope over the ship's edge.

The diver would take a deep breath, filling his lungs with air, then quickly put a peg on his nose to keep his nostrils shut and stop water from entering his lungs. He'd jump into the water and let the weight take him down to the depths as he braced himself against the water's pressure and exposed himself to the risk of hungry sharks. He would then start scooping the oysters into the bucket tied around his neck. When he felt his breath was running out, he would give the rope one or two sharp tugs to signal to his partner on board the ship, who would then draw the rope up as quickly as possible until the diver's face broke through the surface of the waves and he could gulp in precious air, saving him from suffocation.

His partner would then help him reach the ship.

The diver would hold on to a strut on the outside of the ship for a few minutes as he unfastened the bucket and passed it up to his partner, who would empty it into a spot near him and hand it back to the diver, who'd take another enormous breath, replace the peg on his nose, and dive back down to hunt for more oysters. The men would make ten dives, rest for the same amount of time, then start again.

The strain of diving, holding one's breath, and facing the hidden dangers at the bottom of the sea filled the day from sunrise until the moment towards dusk when the captain saw the sun heading for the horizon. Then he would call out: "Time to store the ropes."

At that moment, all the sailors would appear on the ship's upper deck, chanting: "By day we dive, by night we pray!"

A large petrol tanker looms in the distance. The powerboat's movements are easy compared to a heavy sailing dhow. We don't come across any fishing boats, and our boat bobs along on its own, disturbing the silence of the sea. I can hear Abd al-Wahab telling me: "The ports administration has been moved from the Ministry of Transport, and it's now part of the Ministry of Finance."

"What's the Ministry of Finance got to do with the ports?"

"I don't know. That's what I read in the paper."

I keep looking at him, and he asks: "When are we going to arrive?"

"In less than an hour."

Sulayman is still amusing himself by sorting out the fishing lines. I decide to humour him: "Long live Sulayman."

"Long live yourself."

Abd al-Wahab puts down his newspaper, stands up and opens a carton of mango juice, which he offers to me. Then he opens one for himself and a third for Sulayman.

Thanks to the smooth sea, we're making good time.

"Let's choose a good spot this time," Abd al-Wahab says.

"Then you choose the spot," I tell him.

"You're the Captain." He chuckles and moves off.

I was in the prime of my youth when I joined Captain Yusuf bin Issa al-Qutami. My father sent me off with him. "You'll learn from Captain Yusuf the secrets of the sea, and he'll teach you to be a captain."

Thank you, Father, for you were the one who nurtured my passion for the sea.

"Yusuf is the pilot of a ship that takes water and other supplies to the pearl fishing ships up and down the Gulf. With him, you'll learn where to find the pearl diving spots and how to reach them."

I was happy that my father was sending me out with Captain Yusuf, because I already knew him and admired his seriousness.

"If you want to be a captain, you have to be able to make your word law on board the ship. Yusuf won't tell you everything. You'll have to watch his every move, big or small," my father advised me.

I can still remember that day. We set off early one morning on a dhow: me, Captain Yusuf and five men from the Mahra tribe – the captain throwing furtive glances at me the whole time. I didn't have the courage to ask him why he kept looking at me. The breeze was so light it hardly moved the dhow, which barely moved through the sea. But eventually the coast and city disappeared from sight.

I was standing near the edge of the dhow, looking at the rigging, when someone bumped into me and I found myself in the sea. I shouted and shouted, but the dhow kept to her course without anyone noticing me. Suddenly, I found myself swimming among the waves. It was the first time that the sea had got me all to itself. Fear ran through me, but I managed to get free of my dishdasha and lighten myself. I was wearing just my long cotton underpants, alone with the waves and the hot sun, and I had two options – either swim back to shore or to try and swim towards the dhow. It would be difficult to catch up with the dhow. I told myself that, but I was afraid to swim back to shore, since I hated facing people and admitting defeat. I made up my mind: the wind was so light that it hardly moved the dhow, so I was going to swim in its wake. A tingle of fear went through me as I tried to keep the dhow's sail in my line of vision, and I told myself that the captain, or one of the sailors, would miss me and would come back to look for me. I carried on swimming, trying to conserve enough energy in my arms to save myself from drowning. The dhow kept moving away, and the sea around me looked bigger than ever: just me, the waves, the hot sun and the movement of my arms as I swam in a state of fear. If the captain and sailors had not missed me, the dhow would at least stop when it reached the first pearl fishing boat in order to supply it with water or some other goods. Then they would notice I was missing and come back to look for me. I carried on swimming in the hope that I would reach them or they would notice my absence.

I swam, and I swam, and I swam. Fatigue crept up my arms, my breathing was laboured and my throat was gripped by thirst. The sails started to fade from view. Suddenly, another ship appeared. I didn't want anyone on that ship to see me and go around Kuwait saying: Ali, the son of Captain Nasser al-Najdi, fell overboard on his first day at sea and had to be hauled on board by a passing ship. Death would be more honourable. I kept my body and hands under water. I could hardly breathe. I was afraid the boat would plough into me, so I swam a little out of her path. The moment the boat was a short distance away, I went back to the matter at hand, which was swimming. I could feel the fear all around and told myself: "The sea is my friend and will not betray me." At that, a little strength came back to my arms. The full heat of the sun had started to wane. If I were to die, people would say that the Najdi boy died at sea . . . Just me, and the waves, and that dreadful foreboding. My arms grew tired and my breathing laboured, so I swam along on my back to let my arms rest a little.

I kept on repeating: "I'll catch up with al-Qutami's dhow or he'll notice and come back to save me. The fading sun dipped down towards the sea, and then a dhow appeared in the distance. It was al-Qutami's dhow. A little hope and vigour crept back into the beat of my heart. I swam closer and closer to the dhow. I could make out the faces of the sailors as they threw a rope out to me. As I hauled myself back on board, they started calling out: "Hey there! Hey there!"

Someone threw me a dishdasha to cover myself.

"Where were you trying to go?" al-Qutami asked me.

"Back to you."

"And if you hadn't made it?"

"You would've noticed I was gone and come back for me."

One of the sailors offered me some water and dates.

That night, I slept with numb arms and the roar of the waves in my ear.

The next evening, al-Qutami took me aside:

"Not everyone who feels close to the sea can become a captain."

I was listening to him.

"There are many sailors, and few can become captain."

His voice was a little anxious as he said: "If you want to be a captain, you have to give yourself over to the sea and its dangers."

I went on watching every movement of al-Qutami's. He only had to look in my direction for me to rush over and do anything he wanted.

When three months were gone, and only the last month of the pearl fishing season remained, he ordered me to stay seated at the rudder. When we got back to Kuwait, he told my father: "Your son knows a great deal about the sea, Kuwait and the Gulf." He fell quiet for a moment before he turned and addressed me: "I admire your courage, but you'll have to be more careful."

The sea is my friend. It calls out to me, and I follow its call.

I feel the boat gliding along so smoothly it seems afraid to disturb the surface of the sea. Only the sound of the engine breaks the silence.

Abd al-Wahab is taken up with the singing of Shadi al-Khaleej and with his newspaper, while Sulayman is occupying himself with the fishing lines, the tack and the lead weights.

On my second trip with Captain al-Qutami, he took me with him on a voyage. We set out from Kuwait for Basra and finished up at the ports in India. On the night of our return, I was speaking with the helmsman at the rudder and listened to the chief of the seafarers talk about his adventures. Al-Qutami got up and found me awake. He had gone to sleep and woke at dawn to find I had already performed my ablutions before saying my prayers.

On that trip, I would open my eyes and let them be filled by the sea. There was no land to be seen – just the sea and its heavenly mantle. I would read the map and check it against the compass. I would follow the stars and try to make out the sound of the wind speaking with the sails. It was on that trip that I truly realized that the wind was a captain's best instrument. He uses the wind to sail and to reach his destination.

I never ceased my questioning of al-Qutami, al-Mujaddami and the helmsman. I felt a thrill as I learnt the sea routes and the locations of various ports and was able to warn the helmsman of any approaching peril. I would watch how the sails filled with air and the angle they made with the mast and boom. I would sit cross-legged beside the helmsman as we smoked a nargila together and spent evenings chatting away by the light of the compass, with me listening to his tales and asking questions with a passionate heart. As we talked, he kept his hand on the rudder. I would make a note of when the wind changed direction and the dhow along with it. More than once, he asked me: "Don't you trust me?"

"I do trust you, but I want to learn."

On that trip, amid the high black waves, I learned the answer to the question of my childhood: "How does the sea take big ships and make them appear so small?"

Out there, in the vast expanse of the sea, a dhow looked no bigger than a small piece of wood bobbing along in the breeze as the wind and fate amused themselves. There, my soul realised it was a small plank of wood that stood no chance against the enormity of the sea. And it was out there that I saw how grown men tremble, how the fear of death etches itself on the faces of men when the sea becomes angry, and how they call out: "God save us!"

They struggled against the breakers and sensed death seeping under their skins. The only refuge they had out at sea was that of God's mercy.

It was out there, in a moment of lucid thinking, that I made a pact with the sea: "There is no power greater than the sea. You, Ali al-Najdi, will be a righteous son of the sea, and the sea will be your friend."

"When are we going to get there?" Abd al-Wahab's voice brings me back to myself.

I look around before answering: "In less than half an hour."

The sun has filled the sky. I'm standing at the wheel with the compass in front of me. Our boat seems to know its own way as it draws a transient white line on the surface of the sea, creating a wavelet that melts back into the nothingness of its existence, into its watery vastness.

"What's in the paper?" I ask Abd al-Wahab, and he comes over and sits down beside me.

"Nothing new. Khomeini promised to support Arafat . . ."

"It's just words. The only ones who can liberate Palestine are the Palestinians."

"You're right."

I see a few freighters in the distance.

"Sulayman's in his own world over there."

"He never gets bored of getting all the new hooks ready and attaching them to the lines."

"He enjoys it."

"Why aren't you checking the compass?"

"The compass is in my head," I answer, and we lapse back into silence.

I'm standing in the wheelhouse. The sea teaches

sailors patience. The boat speeds on, and there's only half an hour to go.

I look into the distance. The sea takes up my whole field of vision . . . I've been talking to myself . . . I've forgotten all about fishing. It's for the sea that I go out to sea.

Chapter 3

2:30 p.m.

This looks like a quiet spot. I'll turn off the engine. The boat will come slowly to a halt, and the waves around it grow calm.

It's here that the sea is at its most beautiful and expansive. I don't think I'll ever get enough of this glistening expanse around me. When a man falls in love with a woman, he embraces her and breathes in the perfume on her neck. He feels the smoothness of her body and hopes she, in turn, will hold him tight. But how can a man hug the sea or hold it to his chest?

I remember this: We had just moored in Bombay the day Salim dragged himself over to me, eager to talk.

"I need your help."

Salim was one of my favourite sailors.

"Go on." I encouraged him to get the words out.

"I want to get married."

Excitedly, he told me that for the last year he'd dreamed of marrying an Indian girl. He'd become acquainted with her father and couldn't face being separated from her. He said he'd die if he had to go back to Kuwait without marrying her. "Please," he begged, "come with me to the engagement party."

"All right." I smiled.

That evening I put on my best clothes, doused myself with scent and went off with him.

I gladly witnessed the marriage, provided the dowry, and warned him not to mention this to anyone. I held a party with music on board the ship and then, when we got back to Kuwait, I gave him some cash and told him:

"Here's to you and your bride."

The air, when it grazes our skin, has a cold edge to it.

"This is a good spot," I tell Sulayman.

"I hope to God it is!"

The boat slows down and begins its whispering with the sea. Sometimes, I feel as though the sea can bear neither visitor nor resident. Always self-contained, sometimes calm, other times angry, white, blue, brown, green, grey, black, smooth-surfaced or choppy. It is as if the sea cannot stand to come across a human anywhere on its surface or in its depths. I have often wondered if that's why the sea rejects friendship with man. But what harm can it do the sea to befriend a sea captain who is in love with it and who wants to know its world?

We take out the fishing lines and, as usual, we all take

a corner and start untangling the twine. The expanse of calm sea around us takes our minds off everything and, apart from the odd moment of conversation, we could entertain ourselves just by fishing. I enjoy going out with the brothers, Abd al-Wahab and Sulayman, as they are both generally taciturn.

"Let's weigh anchor here," I tell Abd al-Wahab.

"All right."

I leave my spot in the wheelhouse and head for the prow. I heave the anchor, with its wet rope, out of its chest. The hem of my dishdasha grazes the water on the deck, and a slight fish smell wafts up from the boards. I lean over to lower the anchor gently into the water. It slides down, finding its way to the sea floor. I check that the rope is firmly knotted.

"Where's the bait?" I ask Sulayman.

"I've got it here."

He hands me a plastic bag full of bait, and I step over to my spot at the prow, where I start feeding out my line.

"So now we're out here all alone," I say to Sulayman.

"The whole catch will be ours." He laughs, and adds optimistically: "We'll go back with a huge catch."

We're out here in the middle of the nothingness, with only our presence and the silent, heedless sea. Abd al-Wahab casts his line.

I enjoy fishing. Every cast of the line is the start of

an adventure. It's an enjoyable game, a struggle between man and fish, with the man above the water's surface and the fish in its depths. I cast off and brace myself, trying to eavesdrop on the water, where a fish is swimming around the bait, making a cautious approach and then darting away. The world around me fades, and the only thing left is waiting for the line to pulse at the moment when a fish tries to snatch the bait and I try to reel it in. Sometimes I'm aware of a fish lurking around the bait, as if inspecting it or breathing on it. There's a fleeting moment when the fish brushes against the bait and I jerk the line. One of us will win: either the fish grabs the bait and swims off, or I jerk the line and feel the weight of a fish on the hook. Sometimes, if the fish is big and it swallows the bait, I have to outsmart it in order to reel it in.

There's nothing better than this sport with a big fish. I keep the line slack and let the fish swim free so I can surprise it and reel in the line ever so gently, keeping the fish calm and feeling its stubborn resistance. The bigger the fish, the more difficult and delightful the chase. Sometimes I can even see it close to the boat. A nice tender fish, pulsing with life, struggling against its bad luck. Squaring off with a big fish at sea can some-times mean a loss: it might snap the line or, in trying to wriggle free, rip off part of its mouth. I remember once I spent more than an hour and a half trying to reel in a large fish. Often, when I catch a fish, I examine it. I watch as it shakes its bright coat, how it hates to leave the sea, and how it refuses to submit to death. I quickly remove the hook from its mouth and smile as, overcome with joy, I put it back into the sea and tell it: "Thank you. You can go home now."

"Oh God, please," Abd al-Wahab says as he tries to reel in a shiny seabream that's struggling on the line.

"Good, good," Sulayman encourages him.

Abd al-Wahab eases the hook out of the fish's gills, opens the plastic live box, and drops in the fish. Yet again, I can smell the distinct odour of fish.

"There's not much water in the box," Abd al-Wahab tells his brother Sulayman, who scoops up some sea water in a small bowl and empties it into the box.

I feel the tug of a fish on my line. I give it a jerk. I've got one. The line's heavy.

I heave and heave and reel in another seabream.

"Look." I hold up the writhing fish to show Sulayman.

"Fate is with us!"

I place my fingers on its slippery body and eventually manage to work the hook out of its mouth. I hold it up and walk over to drop it into the box. Drops of its blood are smeared on my palm of my hand. I watch as it continues, resolutely, to writhe.

"How long will you go on refusing to get married?" I remember my mother's voice that night. We were in my father's room, stretched out on the blue and red rug that covered the floor. We gathered around the charcoal brazier. The lantern's yellow wick lit up the room as our exaggerated fantasies flickered across the mud walls. We were sipping tea and talking of past trips. For two years, my mother had been trying to get me married off, and I kept repeating my only condition: "I will not marry a girl I have never seen."

At the time, I was perhaps a little more than nineteen. I had returned from a trip to India with Captain al-Qutami just a week earlier. We had stayed there almost six months.

"Ali." Abd al-Wahab's voice got my attention. A two-bar seabream is fighting against his line.

"This is a great spot," I told him. Then I shout over to Sulayman, in jest: "It's cold out here."

He turns around. "We'll warm up when we eat . . . My wife made us an excellent shrimp biryani."

"It sounds delicious."

Sulayman knows how much I appreciate his wife's cooking, and she excels at shrimp biryani – delicious rice mixed with spicy shrimp. Her food reminds me of my mother's.

I can still see my mother's face as she chides me:

"You're coming up on twenty and all your friends are married."

"You know my condition," I interrupt her.

"Oh, son, what's to become of you."

"I won't marry a girl without seeing her first."

"There is no might nor power except in God." She could not contain herself any longer. "How long do I have to go on waiting for you to get married? Why do you torture me?"

"You're a captain now. You have to get married," my father interjected, and I had the feeling that my mother had arranged something with him.

"Your sister Maryam has found you a bride this time," my mother told me.

"Your mother and sister love you a lot," my father said.

"I have to see the girl first," I told my sister Maryam, adding, "don't tell a soul, but bring her here with her mother for a visit, and I'll look at her from afar."

"Shame on you," my mother objected. "You've got sisters."

"It's not forbidden under God's law. Islam allows that," I interrupted, and my father did not object.

"You'll never find a family in Kuwait who'll allow that for themselves or their daughter. And what's more, there's no girl or woman who'll allow her face to be seen by a stranger."

"There's no need for her to unveil her face. I just want to see her for a moment from a distance while she's with you and her mother, and Maryam and my other sisters."

"She's a very sweet girl," Maryam offered. "I know her."

"It's my right to see her, and it's her right to see me, too."

Then came the evening of Shamma's and my wedding. My sister Maryam came to my newlyweds' room in my father's house, with its whitewashed walls, rugs on the ground, cushions and a high double bed. She stood in the doorway, looking at me.

"Come on in," I told her.

"I have a request," she said, in her most loving tone.

"Anything you want." I smiled.

"Are you sure?" She remained standing, her sweet face bright with embarrassment.

"I'm sure, Maryam."

"Don't be irritable with Shamma."

I smiled at her, and she continued:

"You're my brother, and I know your temper."

"I will be calm and good with your friend."

She just stood there, and I assured her: "As God is my witness, I won't break this promise."

"I know how your temper can flare up, but that you're also good-hearted and kind." Her voice rose as she backed away.

"I'll always be there for you."

When evening started to fall, I put on my new dishdasha. I put on my kufiyah and fastened it in place with an agal. Then I put on the formal robe, the *bisht*, wafted incense over myself, and sprinkled myself with my favourite *oud* oil. I put on my new shoes. Then I was surrounded by my father and two brothers, Ibrahim and Abdallah, as well as my close friends from the al-Qutami family and our neighbours the al-Faddalas, the captains and merchants who were friends of my father, and the sailors and my friends from our neighbourhood. The whole wedding group made our procession to al-Adsani's, carrying kerosene lamps while a group of men sang and played tambourines and drums.

My brother Ibrahim shouted out to me in joy: "My God keep evil away from us – your wedding procession is even bigger than mine was!"

May God have mercy upon you, Shamma. At your side, I was blessed with the good things in life. God blessed us with five children. You were the best person I could've entrusted my home and children to while I was away at sea. I remember once I said to Shamma: "You're a captain, too."

She was amused by my statement, and as a smile lit up her face, I explained: "You are the captain of the house."

I would be away six or seven months at a time while she stayed in our family home, bringing up the children, managing their affairs, and watching over them.

The day she died, I was overcome with grief. As I took my leave of her, I tried to hide my tears, whispering to her black-shrouded corpse: "Why, Shamma? Why have you left me all alone?"

Her spirit stayed and lived with me for years, even though I was surrounded daily by a house full of my children and sisters and all their kids. As night fell, the spirit of Shamma would come and be with me. My sisters and children all urged me to get married again so I would have some company in my life. They kept at me to take Noura as my second wife.

"Come on," I hear the voice of Sulayman calling out to me. "Lunch is ready."

I wind in my line. The smell of biryani is all over the boat, rousing my appetite. "You're hungry but you just don't know it!"

Sulayman's words have expressed my inner thoughts. "The smell of the biryani is driving me crazy."

"When you're hungry, your stomach speaks!" he says, teasing.

I sit down with Abd al-Wahab and Sulayman around a plate of biryani and a bowl of thick tomato sauce made with peppers and garlic.

The calm sea is warmed gently by the sun's rays, unperturbed in its loneliness and silence. The boat bobs away in the embrace of the sea's expanse and the cool February breeze.

"I haven't seen any other fishing boats today," I say.

"It's a huge stretch of water out here," Abd al-Wahab says. "Maybe one will come later."

"Maybe."

We sit there in silence, enjoying the delicious food. When food appears, words aren't needed. Sulayman gives me a second helping.

"Praise be to God. I've eaten so much!" I tell him, raising my hand to stop him giving me any more food and leaning back against the chair. "To your health."

I caught sight of the nargila. I was sitting alone in my usual corner in the dhow's stern, and Yusuf al-Shirazi brought it over to me. After the first few delicious drags, I looked at the sailors scurrying around the ship. I turned the other way, and the sea filled my field of vision, glistening, either enshrouded in its darkness or in deep conversation with its moon. It occurred to me that the captains were the young sons of the sea – its offspring giving pride and joy. In the soul of every captain there was a seed of the sea's secret. Everything around me blended into the darkness, leaving me with only the smoke of the nargila. The dhow ploughed along, cleaving the surface of the sea. I felt elated at the thought that there was nothing on earth like being a captain sitting all alone, watching his ship as the wind filled its sails, giving him a feeling of pride and satisfaction.

"I'll make some tea," I tell Abd al-Wahab.

"Captain's tea is excellent," he teases.

I get up to put the water on. I measure out the tea into the pot and pour boiling water onto it.

"You have to go to Dhat Al Salasil bookshop in Salmiya," Abd el-Wahab tells me as he picks up *al-Qabas* newspaper. "The bookshop's advertising a sale of the second part of *Pearling in the Arabian Gulf* by Saif Marzouk al-Shamlan."

"Saif's a friend of mine. I'm sure he'll bring me a copy the next time he comes to visit."

"The advertisement was in the paper last Sunday."

"I like Saif Marzouk's writing. He sincerely loves the sea, and it comes out in his books."

I pour a cup of tea for myself, another for Abd al-Wahab and a third for Sulayman.

"Here you are." I hand them the tea. "Put the sugar in yourselves."

I walk back over, pick up my own tea and head to my corner. I love sipping hot tea and reminiscing in the company of the sea.

Saif writes about the history of pearling. After a few pearling trips with my father, I turned away from the idea of it as a career. The pearling season lasts four months, and the boat moves very slowly. It crawls along from one good pearl fishing spot to the next in search of pearls. The captain stays at his place from sunrise to sunset. He watches over every diver and their valuable haul. The divers fight against hunger all day, having nothing but a few dry dates and sips of coffee until the sun sets and it's time for dinner. Clusters of sailors form around one large plate, and they share a dish of local rice and fish. When night falls, the men fling themselves exhausted into sleep, and every last sound and movement on the boat dies away.

On one such night, I whispered to my father: "I don't like pearl fishing."

As always, he remained calm, looking at me.

"For four months, the captain watches over his divers," I said. "They exhaust themselves gathering oysters all day, and on the next they sit prising them open in search of the ever-elusive pearls. It's a deadly job."

"That's how they earn their bread, son."

I told him of my ambition: "I want to be the captain on a sea-going vessel."

"A sea-going captain must be a friend to the winds and the terrifying adventures, and his comings and goings are all in the hands of God."

May God grant you peace, Father. You spoke the truth.

Father, a sea-going captain in a dhow is indeed a friend of the wind. He knows the seasons when it blows, and he understands the paths it travels. He can hear its secret whispering, and a sixth sense helps him to decipher its rumblings. He rejoices deep inside when the wind arrives, and he becomes anxious and uneasy at its anger. And he feels, along with it, the moments of its mad howling.

A sea-going captain, Father, has naught but God and the wind. He might be sailing in a dhow that can carry a hundred, or even a hundred and fifty tons of freight, yet without a motor and with the help of nothing more than the gusts of wind filling his dhow's sails. He faces the wind with a smile when it blows in the right direction, and his soul flutters with the sails as the dhow cuts through the sea's surface on its way to the long-awaited supply ports. When the wind dies down, he respects its wish and waits through the period of calm. It starts up again, and he steers his dhow along its course. Then the wind begins to rage, tossing the dhow about, and he sets to adjusting the sails, asking God for help, summoning up all he knows, holding the tiller stiff as a rod, and directing the rudder – for he is the captain of sails and men.

A sea-going captain loves the wind as he would a jealous woman who tempts him with her flirtations. It misleads him, and meekly he follows. It rears up at him, and he knows how to satisfy its whims.

Father, a sea-going captain knows the language of the wind like he knows the back of his hand.

"The captain's in his own world over there with his cup of tea."

Abd al-Wahab's voice brings me back to myself.

"He's not with us any more," Sulayman quips back.

"Gone away with my memories," I tell Sulayman.

"I think I know you by now," says Abd al-Wahab. "You come out to sea to be alone with yourself."

"True."

The two men get up, still holding their tea.

"We're going to fish again," Sulayman tells me.

I see a large ship passing in the distance.

"The family will have a great ship, an ocean-going dhow."

The day my father told me that, in his usual calm manner, we were sitting on rush mats in the courtyard, eating mezze: my father, my mother and me. As he continued, my heart fluttered in my chest.

"It will be a dhow used for freight, travel and trade between the ports of Kuwait, Basra and the Gulf, and Aden and the ports of East Africa and India."

I was in my mid-twenties. My father stopped eating and looked straight at me, adding: "You'll go to India and load up with timber and all the other items necessary for boat-building."

I got up and kissed him on the head to show my gratitude. It was clear that my father had chosen me for this job as a sign of his trust in me as a captain, putting me ahead of all the sea captains of Kuwait and the Gulf.

"Are you sailing with him?" my mother asked.

"No. Ali the captain will go with his own men."

In 1937, Muhammad Husayn, the master shipwright, finished building the family dhow. My father called it the *Bayan*.

On its maiden voyage, the experienced sailor Ali bin Husayn helped me, and the following year I steered it alone, feeling a sense of pride and elation. It was then that I thought I might be the youngest captain in all Kuwait and the Gulf.

Towards the end of 1938, I was in Aden, in the port of al-Ma'ala, when the trader Ali bin Abd al-Latif al-Hamd told me: "Alan Villiers, an Australian captain, would like to accompany you on your trip to Zanzibar."

I didn't like the news, nor did I accept the idea. I remained silent, and he added: "The British High Commissioner asked me to help him out."

It was at lunch, seated around the table on the first floor of al-Hamd the trader's office, that I first met Alan, and I was drawn in by his enormous stature and his feline gaze. He stretched out a huge hand to greet me, and I got up to shake it. Our eyes met, and antipathy seemed to rise up between us.

He started speaking with al-Hamd in English, and al-Hamd turned to me and said: "I've told him you're one of the best young Kuwaiti *nakhodas*."

Alan looked at me, as if weighing up the trader's statement, and then he asked al-Hamd: "What does '*nakhoda*' mean?"

Although I couldn't speak English, I understood the question. Al-Hamd replied:

"*Nakhoda* means captain, master of the ship. The person who has complete control over the running of the ship and everyone on her."

They spoke some more in English, and al-Hamd explained to me: "I told him that al-Najdi is a shipmaster who's renowned for his courage, bravery and sense of honour."

"That's a great compliment, coming from you." I smiled gratefully.

"It's true, son of Ali Nasser al-Najdi."

Alan continued to measure me with his gaze. I was getting fed up and turned my face away from him. I think that he got the point.

A question leapt into my mind: "What will this foreigner do on board my ship?"

"He's a captain who has sailed the world in a large motor boat," Al-Hamd said. "He's also a famous writer and photographer."

But what would he make of the way I handled my sailors on board the dhow? The question kept replaying in my mind.

Three days later, Alan came to visit us on board the dhow, which was anchored among the other Kuwaiti dhows in the harbour of Aden. The ship's greatness made my heart flutter with pride and gratification.

That night, I held a large concert and party in Alan's honour. It was an evening saturated by a damp, cool breeze. Lamps lit up the whole dhow, and the deck was covered with Persian rugs. I called al-Mujammadi, the chief mate, and told him:

"Have them start the drumming. I want this to be a night to remember."

I can still remember the lights of that night, and I can still hear the sounds of the party, with its singing and clapping.

I get up to fetch another cup of tea.

"Want a cup?" I ask Abd al-Wahab.

"No thanks. There are going to be moderate north-westerlies with occasional gusts." I look at him, and he adds: "That's the weather forecast in the paper."

"And then what?"

"The swell will vary from light to heavy."

"The swell is very light at the moment," I say before I raise my voice to call to Sulayman: "Tea?"

"No thanks. I've had enough."

That night, we all sat on board, drinking black lime tea with orgeat. When al-Hamd brought Alan with him, I welcomed them both and seated them beside me on the bench at the stern, behind the helm, where they sank down into the high woollen cushions. With a slight smile on his lips, al-Hamd told me:

"It's just like you to have a party at any opportunity."

"There's nothing better than sitting with friends and listening to music."

"Alan visited your dhow yesterday and wrote a description of her."

"I know," I replied.

Alan took out a piece of paper and started reading, while al-Hamd translated for me:

"It towered over all the sambuks and ships in the bay. Her teak mainmast stood ninety feet above the sea and her tremendous lateen yard was made of the trunks of three trees, lashed stoutly end for end with many lengths of canvas-bound rope."

Pride welled up inside me. Al-Hamd continued:

"Alan told me: 'al-Najdi's dhow is enormous yet light, strong yet fast, solid yet sleek.'"

"Did you tell him it was built by Kuwaitis?"

"Of course."

That night, Alan immersed himself in conversation with al-Hamd. Yusuf al-Shirazi took the Arabic coffee around, and the sailors offered trays of sweets, figs and dates.

I was smoking a nargila, listening to the conversations between al-Hamd, Captain Abdallah al-Qutami, Captain Hamed bin Salem and the rest of the traders and shipmasters at the party. We tried to include Alan in our talk by means of al-Hamd when possible.

Ismail al-Qatari sang his mournful tunes to the assembled crowd. The sailors beating *marawees* drums struck them harder, sending their sounds out into the night, over the port, which was still thronged with traders, sailors and workmen. The clapping grew louder, and soon the music moved Abdallah al-Qutami and I to get up and perform the swaying *zaffaan* dance, followed enthusiastically by the young sailors, who were animated by the music that worked its way through their bodies.

As Alan was leaving, he turned to me and spoke with the little Arabic he knew:

"*Shukran jazeelan 'ala ad-dawati.*"

Al-Hamd explained: "Alan has really enjoyed the party. He says that your kindness knows no bounds."

Now, as Abd al-Wahab and Sulayman enjoy their fishing, I was starting to feel a bit numb. I decide to finish my tea and perhaps stretch out for a while.

Alan sailed with us for six months. We set out from Aden towards the end of 1938, and ended up in Kuwait in the middle of 1939. He was a sailor and a sea captain who'd known the terrors of the seas and the oceans of the world, having crossed them in ships, but he'd always been haunted by the tales and adventures of Arab sailors. He told the merchant, al-Hamd:

"The Arab dhows are the last relics of the magic of the old Orient."

He'd come with me in order to discover how sailing ships without motors travelled across the seas, dependent upon no more than the trade winds and the expertise, vigilance and courage of their captains and sailors. I soon came to learn that he had a hidden desire to observe and evaluate an Arab captain.

A sweet numbness weighs down my eyelids.

"I'll just have a little nap," I say, raising my voice to let Abd al-Wahab know.

"You're getting over the hill now, old man" he shoots back.

"The captain's a young man," Sulayman parries.

"But," I murmur, "sleep conquers all."

I leave the fishing line. The boat feels stable, and the anchor is secure. I remain silent for a few moments in case I feel something.

"The weather's fine, and the boat is calm," I say to no one but myself.

I stretch out, an arm over my eyes to keep out the sunlight, and drift into a delicious slumber.

Chapter 4

7:30 p.m.

I feel the slight movements of the boat. The sun had set while I was sleeping. That's not normal for me – I must've dozed for more than an hour and a half. I shouldn't have left Abd al-Wahab and Sulayman and fallen asleep. Noura was right: "You've gotten old, Ali."

"Well, good morning. The fishing's been good today." Sulayman's voice rouses me. I sit up, trying to rub the sleep out of my eyes. I go back to my place, planning to have another cup of tea.

Darkness surrounds the boat. I cast out a fishing line. I notice the cold's sharp sting, perhaps because I've just woken up.

"Yellowfin sea bream, narrow-barred Spanish mackerel, two-bar seabream, and grouper." Sulayman happily tells me the varieties of fish they've caught.

The boat shudders slightly, and I draw back, holding my breath and trying to listen carefully. A small wave is playing around with her. I take the measure of the breeze and then go back to my seat and the fishing line.

I can feel the line tugging in my hand. I pull on it.

It's something heavy. I reposition myself in my seat and then stand up.

"The captain's up." Abd al-Wahab's voice reaches me.

"I've got something heavy here. It could be a sobaity bream, one of those silver-black seabreams," I tell him, feeling the fish fight stubbornly against the line. Sulayman puts down his rod and comes over to me. As he stands beside me, I tell him: "It's a big one, definitely a sobaity. I hope it doesn't snap the line."

"You're the captain. Take it in gently . . . gently."

I try to reel it in calmly, feeling its weight. I notice the darkness creeping over the sea.

"Let's light the lamp."

Sulayman hurries off to light it.

"The fishing's better now," Abd al-Wahab interjects.

I reel and reel. Just me and the line and the obstinate fish. I can feel the fish somewhere near the boat. Its resistance and thrashing are becoming more violent. I haul on the line and relax . . . I'm taking it easy. Abd al-Wahab and Sulayman are both sitting next to me, watching. The smell of fish has grown stronger in the boat and on our clothes. I tug on the line. The fish is close to the surface. I tug again. It appears, thrashing around for dear life. I keep reeling it in.

"That's a big sobaity!" The fish breaks through the water again, and it's a battle between the fish's strength against the strength of my arm. I'm afraid it's going to break the line, and I manage to swing it quickly onto the deck of the boat.

"Well done, Ali," Abd al-Wahab says encouragingly.

"Well done, Captain."

Sulayman bends over to remove the hook from the mouth of the big, pulsating fish. A few drops of blood have spattered on the deck. "Let's share the fish among our family and friends tonight," Sulayman says.

"Sure."

Sulayman holds the fish carefully by the gills as it continues to thrash around. He carries it over to the plastic crate, as its tail scrapes along the deck. As he tosses it into the crate I ask him:

"Is the crate full now?"

"It's a big crate," he replies with a laugh.

"It's been a great night," Abd al-Wahab says.

Sulayman and I go back to our seats. I put bait on my line and cast again.

I grow aware of a strange breeze caressing my face, passing under my nose. It carries a faintly familiar smell. But no, maybe it doesn't. It's February, so it can't be a passing squall or storm. Just now, the fishing has become even better, with sobaity bream right beneath the boat. I check my watch. Quarter to eight. Abd al-Wahab tells me the newspaper is forecasting light to heavy swell. We're in sight of the Kuwaiti coast, which means we aren't far out at sea.

In the days of my boyhood and youth, I learnt to recognise the difficult coasts and ports. We'd set out from Aden, and Captain Alan Villiers was noting down everything that happened on board the dhow. We were heading to the ports of East Africa on our way to Zanzibar and the delta of Tanzania's Rufiji River. On the way back, we made our way to the ports along the southern edge of the Arabian peninsula, the Gulf and then Kuwait. He liked Kuwait, and finished writing his book in al-Hamd's house. It's true that he wrote down everything about our trip, although from his point of view, and with occasional exaggerations and mistakes. Because his book was published in a number of languages, I became quite well known around the world. He set down the events of our trip for posterity, describing the *Bayan* as well as Kuwait's maritime history.

"When will we turn back?" Sulayman asks.

That is maybe the fourth time he's asked, and the question is starting to irritate me.

"This isn't like you," I say. He remains silent, and I ask: "Are you afraid of something tonight?"

"The fishing's great," Abd al-Wahab points out.

"I'm not afraid, but the wind is getting stronger, and it's cold, too." Sulayman gets up from his seat. He comes over and stands between me and his brother Abd al-Wahab.

"Are you trying to escape the cold?" I look at him.

"Are you in a hurry to get home?" Abd al-Wahab asks.

"No. But the wind . . ." Sulayman says in a tone of resignation.

"We're heading back," I tell him. "We're not going to be out here much longer."

"As you wish."

He goes back to his seat, and I go back to my fishing line.

When Captain Alan Villiers and I were together on the dhow, that became my spot on the prow. I allotted a spot to Alan on the bench beside the helmsman at the rudder. From the very first moment he came on board with me, I could feel his passion to know where the ship was and where it was going. From his spot, he could observe the compass all the time and learn the direction in which the dhow was headed. I told him, via a sailor who could speak English: "Please don't get involved in any of the ship's operations."

"I shan't interfere with anything. But please allow me to ask questions from time to time."

"Agreed."

He could never stay in his seat, and he peppered us with questions in his broken Arabic, attempting sentences that made us laugh. He wasn't too thrilled with my commanding tone. He was a little confused by the

Kuwaiti marine terminology and by my orders to the sailors, which were echoed by the captain of the sails, Hamd bin Salim al-Umar, in his sonorous voice, and then by the head sailor. He found it difficult to understand the system of working on the dhow. He seemed irritated by me, and at first disliked Ismail's sea shanties.

I carried on observing him, saying nothing, but gradually he started to see, with an expert captain's sense, that I was running a tight ship and was perfectly capable of dealing with the changing conditions at any moment. He could see how the helmsman at the rudder, the captain of the sails, and the sailors, all followed my orders, picking up on my slightest gesture and doing what was required of them in the best possible way.

By the time nearly three months had passed, and we had reached the midpoint of our trip, he had put his trust in me and the sailors.

"I don't know how all of you work," he said.

I kept looking at him, and he added: "In the West, everybody on board a ship works according to a very strict routine. Everyone carries out his own defined duties, but you . . ." He paused before he continued. "I don't know. Nothing in your uniforms distinguishes you from one another. One word from you, and everyone springs into action. Your men leap all over the rigging as if . . ." A smile snuck across his face. "Your men move with such ease over the rigging, it's as if they were monkeys!"

He was sitting close to us – me, the helmsman, my assistant and the head sailor. He spoke doggedly to us in his broken Arabic, until we could understand what he was getting at, or else one of the passengers would translate his words, when we had one on board who could speak English. Once, he told me: "You're the grandchildren of Sindbad."

When we got back to Kuwait, I hosted a big dinner for him at my father's house, with the pearl divers, the other captains, the traders and some friends. As he stood in the doorway of our house looking out to sea, he told me: "You're alongside the sea, morning and evening. That's why you're in love with it."

The fish stop biting. My line lies untouched in the water. I can feel the wind beginning to rise around us.

"Any nibbles?" I ask.

"Not a thing," Sulayman calls from his spot.

"Should we head home?" I throw out the question, and there is a moment of silence before Abd al-Wahab answers. "Let's give it a little longer."

Noura had chided me: "Don't be late." But fishing is bait for a fisherman.

Calm descends on our powerboat. We're tired. Abd al-Wahab throws his newspaper aside, and Sulayman turns off the casssette player. It's just us, the silence of the sea, the hint of a cool breeze, and the hope of a passing fish. The boat's no more than a small wooden object floating amid the vastness of the sea.

Night colours the sea with secrecy and the gift of silence, and there are no limits to its darkness and depths. Memories gather around me, dragging me with them.

On that day, from his spot in the aft of the dhow, near the rudder, Alan's behaviour was completely out of character. He came over, bright red in the face and visibly emotional, and told me:

"This must be my imagination. It isn't happening, it *can't* be happening." He added, just as enthusiastically: "You're a skilled and lucky captain with brave sailors!"

It was morning, and we were sailing through the Arabian Sea, close to the mountains and the stony promontory of Ras Hafun. The dhow was heavy with freight and further encumbered by the movements of more than a hundred passengers who'd come on board at Aden, Mokalla, al-Shihr, and Hadhramaut, as well as a group of Bedouin from al-Shihr, who'd come on board to take their children with them to Africa. I was next to the helmsman at the rudder, watching the ship's progress. He had to skirt along the sandbank without allowing the dhow to touch the muddy bottom, navigating by the towering rocky outcrops while taking care not to crash into any of them. I noted the direction of the tide around the dhow and followed the direction of the wind from how it filled the sails above. Any miscalculation could cause a collision. I stood behind the helmsman as he turned the rudder, glancing at the compass, at the way the wind was filling the sails, and then checking our course in the water. I could see just how hard it was for the sailors on a deck teeming with a throng of passengers, children and piles of merchandise.

The dhow had to stay on its precise course. I was on tenterhooks, as every moment was fraught with risk and danger. Then I heard the sound of a body hitting the water, followed by a child's terrified scream. Panic raced through the Bedouins, and there was a scream of distress. "My son!"

The dhow lurched from the sudden movement of passengers, whose mood had now turned grim. They were jostling towards the aft of the ship, trying to find the source of the scream and all shouting: "A child, a child!"

Two of the sailors threw themselves into the water.

"Captain, it's my boy," a woman called out, imploring me.

I knew the waters were shark-infested, and I yelled to the helmsman: "Turn the rudder", gesturing with my hand the direction to turn it.

The sudden movement on board made the ship list to the right, and I now shouted at the captain of the sails: "Take the sails down." The men scurried through the mayhem on board, grabbed the ropes, and lowered the mainsail halfway.

"My boy!" The cries of distress were sending the passengers into a frenzy. We'd just about managed to turn the boat so it stood horizontally against the wind, with the fore facing the sandbar and the aft towards the sea. The sailors lashed down the sail. The current pushed the dhow out to sea and towards the rocks, while the wind filled what was left of the sail and blew us towards the mud of the sandbar. In order for the dhow to stay in one spot, the two contenting forces – the current beneath the ship and wind above her – had to be played against each other.

It was impossible to leave a boy to drown. I stood beside the helmsman, all the while watching the panicking Bedouin, who shouted and struggled with mad determination as they tried to reach the aft of the ship and spot the boy in the water, while not losing sight of the bit of the boy's shirt that was still floating along on a wave. I also glanced at the tiller and the compass, kept watch on the sail and the sailors, as well as the singers Ismail and Abdallah, as they swam around in the waves trying to reach the boy, and also kept an eye out for any lurking shark.

My gaze caught the eye of my brother Abdallah and he, the chief sailor, and Yusuf al-Shirazi ran over to uncouple the lifeboat "al-Mashaw".

"Back off!"

I shouted at the Bedouin who were trying to climb onto the aft. I became aware of Hamd bin Salem, my assistant, rushing over to my side and shouting at his men. Yet the excited throng of people trying to get to the aft was stopping the sailors from making their way over to help us. Abdallah bin Salem, a marine corporal, climbed up the rigging, using both hands and feet to reach the top of the mast, and heaved himself along the mainsail, then swung himself down a rope fastened to the aft, thereby reaching the desired spot by moving above the heads of the distressed Bedouin. He was then followed by the rest of the sailors, who formed a barrier and forced the agitated passengers back.

The muddy seabed was a risk to the ship's bulkhead, and the cliffs were waiting to wreak destruction. There were a hundred and fifty people on board, not including the sailors, as well as merchandise and other items. If the ship went down, the sharks would have a mighty feast, and everything I and my family owned would be lost. The news would spread everywhere: al-Najdi had gone down with the *Bayan*. I could see Ismail and Abdallah getting close to the boy. The first mate and al-Shirazi started rowing the lifeboat, along with my brother Abdallah, through the waves to try and reach the sailors and the boy in the water. The Bedouin were starting to panic, and I yelled at them:

"Get away from the edge!"

Hamd stood beside me, shouting at the sailors. I

tightened my grip on a bamboo stick in my right hand. I considered the current and the wind, the mud and the cliffs, the boy, the two sailors in the water, and the sharks – not to mention my brother Abdallah, the first mate, al-Shirazi and the lifeboat. The main sail was half lowered, and the ship was being tossed about. Every second seemed like an eternity. I strode over to the starboard, and a young man rushed towards me. My stick split the air and landed on him. He stopped where he was, and I pushed him back into the arms of his group.

The foul current was pushing the ship towards the cliffs, as the wind did its utmost to push the ship towards the mud.

"My boy!"

I glanced at my brother Abdallah and saw that he'd reached the two men in the water, who were lifting the boy into the lifeboat before they climbed in, too.

A Bedouin man let out an enormous shout: "God be praised!"

The boy and the five men were now in the lifeboat, heading back to the ship. The sea, however, couldn't bear to let the dhow stay in place any longer. The woman was still wailing, and there was still the commotion and yelling from the distressed passengers, the current, the wind, the sails, the compass, and the sailors. I shouted over to the helmsman: "Take her back." And he began to move the rudder. I shouted to the captain of the sails: "Raise the mainsail."

If the wind were to gust and fill the sails, then the lifeboat would not be able to reach us among the waves. We had to contend with rescuing a boy and five men, as well as with the sharks, the cliffs, the stability of the dhow and its load.

"My boy!"

The sailors were shoving the Bedouin back to stop them from all assembling in one spot. I shouted over to the captain of the sails: "Raise the sail."

The wind filled out the sail, and gradually the dhow turned around. The lifeboat was bobbing in the water as the men put every last effort into rowing towards us. The sailors threw ropes down to the lifeboat as the exhausted woman continued calling: "My boy!"

The ship turned a little away from the cliff-cragged coast. The sailors hauled up the lifeboat with the wet, bawling boy in it, and I gave my men a grateful look.

"May God bless you all," I told them proudly.

The wind that was filling the sails enabled the ship to turn around and get back on course. The clamour from the passengers died down, and the Bedouins' anguish turned into delight at the rescue of the boy. The sailors left me and went back to their places and calm descended on the dhow. The woman then came over to speak to me. "You've saved my boy. May God reward you."

I looked around. *Thank God,* I whispered to myself

and the sea. I took a big breath and felt satisfaction spread through me.

I became aware of Alan doffing his cotton cap, telling me:

"I can hardly believe it. You're such incredible sailors!"

I was moved by his praise, and he added: "I'm going to write this scene into my book so the whole world will know of your skill."

"Ali!" I hear Abd al-Wahab calling to me.

A sobaity is throwing itself all over the deck of the boat.

"It's a great spot here," Abd al-Wahab tells me with delight.

"Yes. The fishing's better than ever," Sulayman adds. He walks over to Abd al-Wahab to remove the hook from the mouth of the fish, which is still thrashing around for dear life. Then he drops it into the crate.

I like to see Abd al-Wahab and Sulayman having a good time as they fish together.

Just then, a small hidden and unnoticed current makes the boat bob up and down. The anchor is still submerged in the depths.

Perhaps we shouldn't stay out late. Abd al-Wahab and Sulayman are still fishing away.

I, however, am out at sea in order to enjoy turning over my memories. The sea alone preserves the events of my life.

Alan Villiers irritated me quite a few times when he rebuked me, saying: "You cling to the coastline. It's hardly ever out of your sight. Arab sea captains avoid sailing out into the open sea."

I was offended by this unjust and incorrect opinion about Arab sailors. I spoke on the subject with him many times, but he stuck to his conviction.

I remember well that trip. We were out at sea, having left Zanzibar on our way to the southern coast of the Arabian Peninsula. Out in the middle of the sea, there was no coast for a captain to navigate by, and it was night. I read the map and calculated the distance between our current position and Ras Asur. The locations were engraved upon my brain. I knew that the current was in our favour, so I was using the mainsail. Alan was still observing me, watching how I made my way to the coast. It was clear that he was worried and unhappy about the use of the mainsail.

"Be careful," he told me. "It's dangerous to use the mainsail in this wind, not to mention that it's night." He fell silent for a while before adding, in a worried tone: "I don't know why you don't like keeping on the ship's lamps at night.

I turned and told him: "You'll see the islands of Abd al-Kuri within two hours."

He made no response, but threw me a glance I didn't

understand, so I added: "God willing."

He remained silent, but the look of worried concern still showed in feline eyes, as if he was trying to recall his round the world trip on his ship, the *Conrad*. I gave my orders to the helmsman. I rechecked the compass, and the dhow continued to move through the darkness, cutting across the water on its way to the coast, the sails full of wind. I stayed awake and alert for any treacherous winds. As I was waiting to draw near to a coast, my heart beat faster and sleep flew from my eyes. I could feel the pulse throbbing in my temples.

There were three of us behind the rudder – Alan, the helmsman and me. Although I was sure of my actions, he was waiting for me to make a mistake. It was dark, and only the sound of the ship broke the silence as it ploughed through the sea under the faint light of the moon. When I caught sight of the tip of the Abd al-Kuri islands, my spirit lifted, and I let out a sigh of thanks to God.

"We'll get there on time," I told Alan.

He remained silent for a while before answering. "I don't know how you do it. I think you must just have the sea lanes carved into your mind."

I stay in my spot at the bow of the boat, fishing line in hand. Where is this wretched wind coming from? Perhaps it is time to start heading home. Have you started to fear the sea, Ali?

I didn't think the wind was going to rise – not in February. Also, we're in sight of Kuwait's shore.

The weather remains clear, even though I recognise the start of a familiar foul wind. Abd al-Wahab and Sulayman are still fishing away. I'll remain alert.

With the outbreak of the Second World War, and the torpedoing of a number of boats, commercial shipping in the Arab Gulf came to a halt. Moreover, the Japanese discovery of synthetic pearls put an end to the attraction of pearl diving. Then, after the export of the first consignment of oil from Kuwait in 1946, the people of Kuwait left the sea: the captains, the pearl fishers, the traders, the divers, the boat builders and the sailors. Everyone turned their backs to the sea and went off to look for work with the oil companies, in commerce or with the new foreign agencies.

The sea was abandoned to its own devices, and I also turned in on myself. I didn't show anyone my pain, but kept looking out to sea and repeating: "You're my destination, and I wouldn't know where else to go."

During that period, I was walking along the beach, looking at the boats as they lay forlornly abandoned on their sides on the sand. As the pain within me increased, I whispered in despair: "The dry land is going to eat up their decks, and the wind will blow through their sides."

Heartbreak gnawed away at me: the sea was no

longer the sea, and the boats now were not the dhows of old.

I sat there, resigned. I held onto a fishing line, having anchored in one port and ready to move off to another, as if I'd been born just to travel with the wind and its dangers.

Abdallah al-Qutami once told me, having listened to my complaints: "You'll be a captain as long as you live."

When the pearl fishing and sea transport work came to a halt, the Kuwaitis' boats were sold to the people of the Gulf, Oman and India. Other boats were stripped, their wood salvaged for buildings or used as firewood. My crew of sailors and I were left with no one to buy our labour. We became workforce fodder for the companies and traders in the new city. The oil companies swept up the sailors as employees, and the traders ran off to find work with the large and small western commodity companies, or else they set up their own. New civil service branches were established to absorb the new workers. A new type of life and people emerged, with new morals and social rules. Yet I, Captain Ali al-Najdi, friend of the sea, had only my dignity and my skill at seafaring, trading, and my knowledge of the wind and sails.

In order to keep on working, I replaced the sails with a motor on one of my dhows, and I took up transporting goods to the ports of the Arab Gulf and India.

Yet in the aftermath of the Second World War and the partition of India, this type of commerce fell into a recession and a new trade emerged: smuggling gold. This was fraught with adventure and risk and the prospect of huge profits. I felt lost, and whenever I looked around me, all I could find was a city I no longer knew, its face sadly and quickly turning into a grotesque painted cement monstrosity. I tried my hand at a few commercial operations, but success did not smile on me. I kept repeating: "A real sailor has no life apart from the sea." I reminded myself that yesterday had gone and that life would never turn and go backwards.

From the moment my eyes opened, I was in love with the sea, and this love has never ceased. It's as if I were born from the loins of the sea and have lived in a permanent state of yearning for it. Sometimes, I ask myself: How could a man whose life is so tightly bound up with seafaring and adventure ever be satisfied with one-day fishing trips? I would go out to sea with my friends, but while they were there for the fishing, I was out there to relive the most beautiful memories of my life.

The sea is enveloped in silence. There's nothing but the darkness, a slight chill in the air, and the small lamp of our boat. Abd al-Wahab and Sulayman are both absorbed in the pleasure of fishing.

"Shall we head back?" I ask Abd al-Wahab.

"The fishing's just getting good now," he says.

"Half an hour more," Sulayman suggests.

"Agreed."

By the end of the forties, the Kuwaiti captains had begun to sell their dhows. I carried on going to gaze at mine, the *Bayan*, which was anchored just offshore, in front of our house, in my father's small boatyard. I couldn't imagine selling her.

My brother Ibrahim said: "The boat doesn't just belong to you – it belongs to the family. So what are you going to do with it?" I just went on looking at him, and he continued: "You won't be able to find any sailors to work with you."

He continued at some length, mentioning how God had opened the door of economic ease to us Kuwaitis. We were no longer obliged to go out to sea and confront its life-and-death terrors. He went on and on and on. Even my younger brother Abdallah shared his views. "I'm not going to work at sea, and I won't get on a boat."

I carried on looking at the *Bayan* from the distance. One night, I went on board and sat behind the rudder. I could see the faces of the sailors, hear their singing and smell their nargilas. I became aware of the mast standing there, all alone, and held it taut with its dry ropes. I could see the sails smiling, full of wind. I could hear the waves crashing against the sides of the dhow. I could see the lights of the ports beckoning to me, and a sense of happiness spread through me. I rushed off to meet Shamma and my children, having returned from India.

I sat there behind the rudder, trying to swallow my pain. I was grieving over Kuwait, pearl fishing and sea-faring. I was grieving over Captain Ali al-Najdi and over the sea itself. I was enveloped by the darkness and immobilised by nostalgia. I made myself comfortable on the chair and passed my fingers over the rudder and the compass. I stood up and wiped my palm over the wood of the mast, resisting the urge to hug it. Dragging my feet through the darkness, I took leave of my ship.

The following morning, I told Ibrahim: "I'm going to make a trip, and it's up to you what you want to do with the *Bayan*. I'm not going to hang around and watch part of my life being sold off."

In 1967, Alan Villiers made a visit to Kuwait along with his wife, and he spent a few days visiting his old friends. When we were sitting together he admitted to me: "Kuwait has changed a lot. It's become a modern city." As he lifted up his now age-worn face, he continued quietly: "Unfortunately, you've divorced yourselves from the sea. There's nothing left to keep you together."

I was too inhibited to pour out my heart to him, but I wanted to say: "Oh, Alan, oil has changed absolutely everything. Alan, I've been experiencing such a dilemma. The only way I know to earn a living is from the sea. Oh, Alan, how can a child of the sea turn against his father?"

I feel an odd swell buffet the side of the boat. Abd al-Wahab and Sulayman are still off in their own world, with their fishing rods. Out of the darkness, that foul smell leaps up and surrounds me.

Chapter 5

10:00 p.m.

"Storm!" I shout like a madman, at the top of my voice. Within a few moments, the foul-smelling wind is around me, choking and suffocating. I jump up, as if stung by a scorpion: "Storm!"

It feels as if a black wind is dragging the boat from below. It is ten at night. I know this accursed wind. I felt its presence around us as, stealthily, it surrounded our position. It started off by skirting the surface of the slumbering sea, nudging it awake. A hateful wind.

"Leave the rods," I yell to Abd al-Wahab and Sulayman.

This wind is treacherous. It will take only a few minutes for it to turn into a fury.

"Quick now, it's a storm."

It's up to me to trust my experience and get the boat back to shore.

"The anchor!" Abd al-Wahab shouts.

There isn't enough time to raise the anchor.

"Quick. Get a knife and cut the rope."

I'm at the anchor chest. I hold the rope while Sulayman tries to saw through it with a knife.

The wind starts to rise around the boat, causing a heavy swell.

"Quick."

"Ali," Abd al-Wahab's voice has an element of panic in it. "The wind is strong."

We cut the anchor rope. I turn quickly and my feet slip out from beneath me, and I fall onto the deck. Shakily, I manage to get back on my feet and head for the wheelhouse.

"Hold on."

"God help us all." I hear Abd al-Wahab's voice.

"I told you both." Sulayman's comment is directed at me, but I ignore it.

I start the motor and sit down at the wheel. Something is unnerving me. You're a friend of the sea, Ali, I tell myself. I'm in the cabin at the wheel. Before me is darkness, but the map of the coast is in my head. I know the route better than the lit-up compass, and I will not stray from it.

Escape . . . The storm will raise a black whirlpool all around us. I have to get out of the path of the eye of the storm. If the storm manages to close around us, then it will be very difficult to break free.

It's a powerful blow. If you survive, Ali, this will change your life.

The wind, which has been stroking the surface of the sea, begins to rise. The stronger it becomes, the choppier the sea will be. My plan is to get away from the storm before it strengthens, before it can lay its black snares before me.

The storm seems to be aware of my attempts to flee it, and it gusts headlong at the boat, trying to throw us off course. The boat shakes and lists forward. "Stay on your guard," I yell at Abd al-Wahab and Sulayman. "Keep holding on tight."

I won't let the coast of Kuwait out of my sight. I can reach it from any direction.

While we were chasing fish, the sea had been stalking us. The frenzied wind has taken me by surprise. It had been waiting for darkness to fall. It used our preoccupation with fishing as its bait, and now it is shrieking out its presence, summoning other winds to join it. It blows angrily, as if it were seizing a precious catch. It is blowing us off course. Ours is the only boat out here, which is why the winds have singled us out. If I try to go faster, we will capsize. I curse the appearance of this foolish rain. The wretched storm has been roused, and now it calls upon the black sky to come down and help it.

I know all about the surprise storms and turns of weather that hide under a cloak of darkness. They pick out a man and, treacherously, they latch on. They summon all their powers and wreak their vengeance on him.

Yes, sea, you know me. Al-Najdi will neither weaken nor give in to a storm. I am seventy. I was born from your loins and raised in your lap. I am a son of the Sharq. I am the fearless shipmaster. I am your friend. I am a creature of the sea and have lived more of my life crossing the seas and oceans than I have on land.

Abd al-Wahab and Sulayman stay close to me. The wind is growing stronger and the swell higher. Black rain is sheeting down. The boat shakes. I know this accursed wind. It howls in order to spark the sea's pride, which returns the favour with enormous waves. The storm knows how to play the sea, and the sea fulfils its wish by matching the storm blow for blow. It can toss the largest ships about and crush them with its games.

I'm not afraid that any sails could be destroyed. The boat starts to list even more.

"God preserve us." I hear Sulayman's voice. "It really is a strong storm."

I grip the wheel with both hands to keep the boat steady. I try to steer so that the waves hit us sidelong and we pass through them.

Water starts pouring onto the boat from every direction.

"Not too fast, Ali," Abd al-Wahab calls to me. He and Sulayman are sheltering in the wheelhouse.

The wind drives the rain, hurling black water down onto the wheelhouse.

The water seeps in. The noise of the wind fuses with

the pummelling of the rain, the roar of the waves, the movement of the listing boat and the darkness. I feel a pain in the small of my back and my knee.

Fear of the storm has driven Sulayman and Abd al-Wahab into a state of lethargy, and they stand stiffly beside me.

"Are we going the right way?" Sulayman asks.

"The right direction is getting out of the storm."

"God preserve us," Abd al-Wahab says, his voice imploring.

The wind is blowing in from all directions, and a window of darkness stands in front of me. I see almost nothing. I point the boat towards the shore. A captain does not need daylight or a compass. I can steer a boat blindfolded. But the furious wind, the mad rain and the ever-rising sea are doing their utmost to confound me.

The storm prevents me from making any progress and forces me into smaller and smaller circles. The more the boat moves, the tighter the storm's grip. The storm is blowing the boat backwards and doing its best to capsize it. The storm urges the sea on to help it destroy us. The elements of nature have united with each other against humanity.

You have already experienced moments of death, Ali. This is not the first time you have battled a storm. During trials like this, a captain must harness all his courage and experience.

"What can I do to help?" Sulayman asks.

"Nothing."

The sky descends to draw mountains of darkness around us. The wind, waves and rain all buffet us.

Right in the middle of some quiet fishing, this storm took us by surprise. It's blowing in from all directions. In the blink of an eye, the djinn of the wind brought rain, high waves and a mountain of darkness, such that the sky fell onto the surface of the sea, leaving us no way out. Even if a storm arrives during the hours of daylight, it can be strong enough to frighten away the light, which is quickly replaced with darkness.

I should have trusted the message of that foul smell and returned to the shore. Sulayman asked us to head back several times. If only I'd gone back sooner . . . The waves are breaking against the boat, beating against the sides of its prow and soaking us.

The cool February breeze has turned into a mad storm.

"When will we reach the shore?" Sulayman asks.

"Let's get out of the storm first."

"Go faster," Abd al-Wahab suggests.

"I have to keep at a steady speed to avoid capsizing the boat. Speed isn't the issue here. The wind is pushing us harder and harder, and the waves are getting higher."

"I told you both," Sulayman repeats with a tone of reproach.

His words feel like a slap. I have nothing to say now.

I tighten the agal around my kufiyah. This is a strong storm, and it's cold, Ali. My dishdasha is soaked and greasy, and my back aches.

A new trial for you at the age of seventy – this isn't how you imagined things. The sea wants to frighten you.

The spray from the waves is now blowing onto us from all directions, as is the cold.

I'm not going to say a word or put the fear into the hearts of the men.

"Stay together," I say, as a form of warning.

"God protect us," Abd al-Wahab says with alarm.

It's unbelievable that I could drown so close to Kuwait's shore.

I steer through a gap in the dark waves, clinging to the wheel so I can bring the boat through the next wave. I hear the crate of fish rolling around. The boat is shaking.

The boat is a small toy, caught inside a treacherous storm that is wailing in the darkness.

I should have listened to my premonition, should have taken notice of the foul smell and Sulayman's requests to head home. Oh, Ali, you're not that young man any more who can stand up to the sea! We'll be lucky if we get through this storm.

"The wind's heavy and the waves are against us."

"Slow her down," Sulayman tells me.

"We're going slowly – it's the storm!"

If I keep the speed down and the boar upright, it will capsize. If I increase the speed, it will capsize.

You're the captain, Ali. The captain alone is responsible for the souls of the sailors and the safety of the ship. Sulayman complained of the cold at the start of the trip. Now, Abd al-Wahab is standing, glued to me, as if seeking protection in my sailing expertise.

"Strange," Sulayman says, "how the weather can turn in an instant."

The prow rises and falls. The angry waves are now higher than the wheelhouse. The wind is trying to capsize us as the high waves beat down on the glass of the wheelhouse.

"God preserve us," Abd al-Wahab yells in horror.

I had been worried that the windscreen would break. And now the waves have the glass, and water is pouring in, both from the waves and from the driving rain. The wind and the water are testing the wheelhouse and the prow. My clothes are soaked.

"Let's put on our lifejackets," Sulayman suggests.

"Bail out some of the water first," I say, my voice rising with the urge to justify myself. "The lifejackets can hinder our movements."

We are still amid the mountains of darkness and wind. The boat continues shaking, now with its broken windscreen.

The boat's lamp is flickering. I keep one hand on the

wheel as I try to pull off my heavy, waterlogged winter dishdasha. I throw it down and shout: "Come on. Start bailing so that the boat doesn't sink."

I turn off the motor. Abd al-Wahab grabs a container and starts bailing. I look for another container. The biriyani pot will be good — I run to it. The prow has filled with water and now it's listing in the angry waves, the rain and the darkness.

Abd al-Wahab, Sulayman and I scoop up water and throw it back overboard. The rain continues bucketing down above our heads and the waves are coming from all sides.

"Have you turned off the motor?" Sulayman shouts over to me.

"Yes."

The storm is doing its merry dance, turning us and the boat into its playthings.

The sea has turned against me in my seventieth year. Why, my friend?

We bail out the boat, with the sea growing ever angrier, the rain harder and the dark deeper.

Our attempt to flee the storm annoys it, and our resistance just provokes it further, as if, at this moment of confrontation, nature is wreaking vengeance on mankind.

"God have mercy on us!" I hear Sulayman call out.

The prow starts to even out.

I want to turn on the engine. I stumble through the

water and floating objects to get the wheelhouse. What if I can't turn on the motor? What if water has got into the motor itself?

"Sulayman," I call to him. "Check the motor."

The boat is listing. I try in vain to get the motor running.

"Come over here!" Sulayman shouts to us from the aft. Abd al-Wahab and I stumble our way over to him through the madness of the water. The engine is waterlogged.

"God save us all," Abd al-Wahab said in a weak voice.

"Let's get the water out of it."

The storm has strengthened, as the waves have grown higher and the rain fiercer. The crashing waves want to break the boat.

"What are we going to do?" Sulayman asks me.

"We going to bail out of the engine, and then we'll try to get the motor running."

I wanted to say, "And if we can't . . ." but held back to forestall Abd al-Wahab's collapse. *You have never once given up,* I tell myself.

"Don't go out to sea," Noura had told me. "Stay at home with us today."

I couldn't help myself, Noura.

A vicious wave strikes the aft of the boat, followed by a second giant wave. Water is seeping in.

"The boat's going down. It's going to sink," Abd al-

Wahab yells in horror.

The aft is quickly going under.

"We'll have to abandon ship!" Sulayman shouts.

Mad waterfalls are streaming onto the boat from all directions.

At the thought of sinking the boat, the storm makes ear-shattering whoops of joy.

We fumble around in the dark.

Why? Why, dearest sea? I'm your friend!

"Whirlpool!" I yell to the others.

"The whirlpool's going to take us down. Get off the boat before she takes you with her."

The boat's lamp goes out, and darkness is upon us.

"Quick. Jump overboard and swim quickly away. The whirlpool around the boat will drag down everything around it. Hurry!" I yell to Abd al-Wahab and Sulayman.

The boat's fittings are now howling from the storm and the wind.

"Lifejackets!" screams Sulayman. With panicked glances, we feel around in the muddy darkness. The aft is going down. Water is now rushing at us from all sides.

"Stay together!" I shout at them. "We throw ourselves overboard and swim off together."

"Quickly!"

Sulayman jumps overboard. I look in the direction of Abd al-Wahab. I can see nothing in the darkness. I shout to him: "Get away fast!"

"Get off the boat. We're over here!" I hear Sulayman's voice calling to me.

Something is holding me back. A captain does not abandon ship.

"Come on!" shouts Abd al-Wahab.

"For God's sake, Ali!"

"Hurry!"

The armies of water and darkness surround me, and I hurl myself into the water.

The waves and the wind toss the boat around. It's going down. The darkness swallows our lifejackets.

I hear Sulayman call out: "Let's swim away from here!"

We swim blindly through the darkness, away from the boat.

"Faster, guys," I shout into the void.

The fish crate floats along near me, and I grab it and shout: "I've got hold of the fish crate. Come over here."

Abd al-Wahab and Sulayman swim over to me.

None of us can see the others.

"Grab onto it. Grab hold!" I yell at them.

"Let's dump the fish."

I feel as if the sobaity are gloating. Abd al-Wahab gets hold of the crate and Sulayman swims towards it.

"Everyone take an edge," I tell them.

There is nothing but the wind, the waves, the rain,

the darkness and the cold water. I have nothing to protect my body except my long cotton underwear.

"The weather's cold out there," Noura had told me. "Don't go out."

"Keep hold of the crate," Sulayman calls.

The sea swallows the boat, and the last traces of it are covered by darkness. The waves toss the contents of the crate around, throwing them against our bodies. The sea is reclaiming its fish. Three heads bob above the water. We are three ghosts, forming a circle around the crate, in the midst of the darkness, the wind, the waves, the cold and the rain.

The sky descends, settling right above our heads. The waves try to snatch the crate from our hands.

At seventy, the storm is trying to devour me!

Abd al-Wahab is close in age to my age, and Sulayman is perhaps five years younger than the two of us. There are things we shouldn't be doing at our age!

"We have to stay together," I tell Sulayman and Abd al-Wahab, and my voice sounds hoarse.

It feels as though the sky is touching our heads. As though, if I were to raise my arm, I could touch it.

Nothing is left of the boat.

"Oh God, treat us kindly," Abd al-Wahab intones.

The storm celebrates wildly. It has sunk the boat, and now it has us to itself. The flimsy crate is all we have to hold on to.

All that time the sea was calling out to me – "*Come*"

– it was setting a snare for me.

I look up at the sky and see nothing but darkness, and the driving rain scours runnels in my face.

Yet however much the wind tries to play with me, I have the coast engraved in my mind. Since I was small, I have never been afraid of the dark, and I know how to cleave a path through it.

The storm will certainly die down, and I will make it back to the shore with my friends.

Chapter 6

10:30 p.m.

We are now some distance from where the boat capsized. When the storm dies down, the lights will appear along the coast, reassuring us, and the outline of the coast will grow clear. For sailors, light is a sign of life.

I am not going to lose Kuwait.

I hope the storm won't last much longer.

"How long has the storm been going?" Sulayman asks me.

"It started up at ten. About half an hour."

"How long do you think it will keep on?" Abd al-Wahab asks.

"God knows." I sigh.

Our rigid fingers clutch the edge of the bobbing fish crate.

Our bodies are submerged in the water, and the black waves strike us from all sides.

"I'm going to die." I could hear Abd al-Wahab moaning through the darkness.

"Just think of God, my brother," Sulayman barks back at him.

"The storm's going to die down."

"My dishdasha's soaked, and it's pulling me down."

"We'll get it off you," Sulayman says. "Hold tight to the crate."

"Ali and I are going to try and get you out of it."

Abd al-Wahab will be like me and Sulayman, naked except for his long underwear.

"We'll rip it open at the neckline. That'll make it easier to get it off you," I shout at Abd al-Wahab. He agrees.

We're talking into the darkness. We speak without seeing each other's faces.

I think of my agal and remove it. It can be used as a rope. I raise my voice and address Abd al-Wahab: "Don't let go of the crate. I'm going to tie my agal around your wrist, so hold on to it while Sulayman gets your dishdasha off you."

The crate is bobbing wildly with the waves, trying to shake us off. I grab Abd al-Wahab's wrist and feel him giving me his arm. I wind the agal firmly around it.

"Sulayman," I say, still unable to see anything. "I've secured Abd al-Wahab's arm and I'm holding onto him. Get his dishdasha off him."

The cold air slaps our faces with rain.

Sulayman is pulling his brother's dishdasha off him as we're tossed around with the crate.

"God give me strength!" Sulayman calls out as he pulls the dishdasha off Abd al-Wahab's compliant body.

One end of the agal is around his arm, and the other is looped around my hand.

"Grab the neckline of his dishdasha," I tell Sulayman.

"We'll each pull in our own direction."

Why, O sea?

I told my father: "The sea's my friend."

My mother had said: "What a load of nonsense!"

I let go of Abd al-Wahab's hand and shout to him: "Hold tight to the crate!"

I grope around for the neck of his dishdasha and tell Sulayman: "Let's tug on it together. You to your side, me to mine."

When sailors tug on the rigging, they do so as one man.

I stretch out my hand to feel for the dishdasha's neck opening. I cannot see Abd al-Wahab's face. I grab the front of his dishdasha.

"Pull!" I shout at Sulayman, and I tug hard on the dishdasha. The crate wobbles, and Abd al-Wahab moves towards me. The neckline of the dishdasha starts to rip. That's a bad omen, I tell myself.

"Slide your arm out," Sulayman yells at his brother Abd al-Wahab. The cold is starting to grip my shoulders, neck and head. My back hurts from when I fell.

"God have mercy on us!" Abd al-Wahab pleads. He leans against the crate as he yanks his arm out of the sleeve. The edge of the crate is going under.

"Don't worry about the crate," I tell him, feeling for the agal wrapped around his arm. If Abd al-Wahab lets go of the crate, he'll drown.

"I can't get my other arm out." Abd al-Wahab's voice pleads with me.

The heavy, sodden winter dishdasha is pulling us all down into the deep.

"I'm going to slip the agal off your wrist. Hold tight to the crate with your other hand. Then I'll be able to get you out of the dishdasha."

I slide the agal off while trying to keep Abd al-Wahab close. I slip it around my neck so I don't lose it.

The storm is still in the depths of its madness, and there is nothing but darkness, rain and waves, and the weight of the winter dishdasha on my arm.

Noura said: "You're not as young as you used to be."

I try to free Abd al-Wahab's arm from the dishdasha. The crate wobbles. I get the dishdasha off his shoulder and feel it slide off him.

"Get your hand out of it!" I yell. The dishdasha comes off. I let go, and it disappears into the darkness of the sea.

Abd al-Wahab is now wearing only his long underwear. The black waves slam into us from all directions.

"Keep hold of the crate," I tell Abd al-Wahab.

"What are we doing to do?" His question blurs into the darkness.

"We're going to hold onto the crate until the storm has passed."

"We'll die of hypothermia," he says in despair.

"We're not going to die. I spent a whole night on the lifeboat al-Mashaw."

"Enough about death," Sulayman objects. "It's a storm. It'll pass."

"An hour ago, the sea was calm . . ."

"We should've headed back earlier," Sulayman interrupts me with his lament.

"I asked you two . . ." But I swallow the rest of my sentence.

I'm not going to blame anyone. "It's my fault."

"It's the will of God, my brother," Sulayman says, clearly trying to make me feel better.

The storm is growing stronger. The waves are even higher, and we cling to the crate that was thrown free of the boat. Cold rain hammers down on our heads.

"All we have left is the mercy of God," Abd al-Wahab says.

"We've just got to keep hold of the crate until the storm dies down," Sulayman tells him.

"And when's that going to be?" Abd al-Wahab asks again.

"Not long. These storms come from nowhere and disappear."

Abd al-Wahab once told a gathering of men: "When I'm with the shipmaster, I don't have to think about anything." He was talking about his sea voyages, and showing how much trust he had in me. "Ali is a creature of the sea!"

Oh, Abd al-Wahab. That shipmaster, that creature of the sea, is now dangling in the darkness while clutching a fish crate.

The wind is growing stronger, and I don't think it will calm down any time soon, but I keep that to myself.

You have lived through many trials on the sea, Ali. But you weren't old then.

"The storm will pass and we'll be rescued," I yell out, as if addressing myself.

"If we swim holding onto the crate, which way should we head?" Sulayman asks me.

"We're near Jelieh." I look up at the sky, and the darkness and water fall straight into my eyes, suffocating me. The storm is trying to test me. I have the coastline in my head: "The moment the storm stops, we'll be able to head towards the shore," I tell Sulayman.

"But when?" Abd al-Wahab repeats his irritating question, and I ignore it.

The sky seizes our breath, suffocating us. Only our heads are above water, and they are battered by the rain and the wind.

Oh Lord, if you want to take one of us, take me. I am Ali bin Nasser al-Najdi. How will I be able to face the people of Kuwait? Let me have an honourable death. Dear God, don't humiliate me in my old age.

My father said: "The sea befriends no one."

Yet I was not expecting a treacherous storm in the middle of February.

I know these dark moments. Every lifetime has its moment, and every such moment brings death.

"I've started shivering from the cold," Abd al-Wahab complains.

"Don't weaken, my brother," I tell him, adding: "If you weaken, you'll take us with you."

"Stay strong, brother!" Sulayman calls out.

I am afraid that Abd al-Wahab will drown. I'll retie the agal around his arm, fixing the other end to the handle of the crate. If his body gives up, or he no longer has the strength to hold on, he'll still be attached to the crate. I unwind the agal from my neck.

"Give me your arm," I tell him. Between us, there is only darkness and rain. The waves toss the crate around, and us along with it.

"I'm going to tie your arm to the handle."

"No." He rejects the thought. "If I drown, I'll pull the crate down with me."

"There won't be any drowning," I growl.

We shout at each other blindly in the darkness as I grope around for his arm. His right arm is hanging on to the crate. Somehow, I will wrap the agal around his arm.

"You have to come over towards the handle," I tell him, and add quickly to Sulayman: "We've got to turn the crate so the handle is close to Abd al-Wahab."

Abd al-Wahab is out there in the darkness, giving up the ghost. Why, Ali, do you shout at Abd al-Wahab when he is paralysed by fear and fatigue?

The wind is howling around us.

"Hang on," Sulayman says. "The storm is growing stronger."

The crate sways as we hold it, filling up with water.

I'm holding the end of the agal so I can tie it to the handle. I don't want my friend Abd al-Wahab to drown. We haven't seen any other boat since we arrived. But even if a boat were to pass by, no one would see or hear us.

"How long are we going to be out here?" Abd al-Wahab returns to his painful question.

"The storm will die down," I say.

"Look!" Sulayman's voice calls out from the darkness.

"A light. A float – a buoy!"

I focus in on it. "That's the marker for the district of Jelieh."

"God be praised," Sulayman shouts with delight, and adds: "Let's try and get over to it."

"It's far."

"We can swim towards it," Sulayman says enthusiastically.

I feel for the movement of the waves and wind. In what direction will it be easiest to swim? How will Sulayman manage to reach the marker in all this wind and rain and swell?

"You have to swim this way," I yell, drawing an arc in the direction of the wind, but the darkness swallows up my gesture. I shout at him: "It's not going to be an easy swim."

"I'm going to let go of the crate and swim," Sulayman shouts.

"Keep the marker in your sight," I tell him. "We're going to be right behind you."

"Here I go," Abd al-Wahab says.

O God, treat him kindly!

"Are you up to swimming?" I ask. "Wait. I'll undo the agal."

My hand fumbles around for the agal.

"Aren't you coming with us?" Sulayman asks.

"I'm going to keep hold of the crate and swim behind you. If either of you gets tired, swim back toward me."

"If we can get onto the marker, come with us."

"The important thing is you save yourselves," I shout.

Abd al-Wahab's hand is now free. I reach out to grab Sulayman's hands.

"Stay strong."

"God protect us," he says despondently.

The black waves are tossing the crate around more than ever. "Let go of the crate one at a time," I tell them. "And swim close to each other."

The waves, the wind and the darkness might separate them.

"We'll swim together. Swim close to me," Sulayman warns Abd al-Wahab.

I look towards the light on the marker. From this distance, I can see it moving up and down. It will be difficult to climb onto the marker. The sharp barnacles and coral growing on it will slash anyone who tries to climb on, and the smell of blood will attract sharks.

"I'll be close to you, holding on to the crate."

"I put my trust in God," Sulayman says as he lets go of the crate. No doubt he hears me uttering, "Forgive me, friend."

Abd al-Wahab follows, and I can make out Sulayman's voice saying: "You're forgiven, Ali."

The black sky clings to my head, and I'm alone with the movements of the crate, which is tossing me around.

They have swum off a little, and I cannot make out their bodies in the darkness.

I paddle with one hand in order to stay near them. I'm worried about Abd al-Wahab.

The crate thrashes around, trying to throw me off.

I paddle with one hand. The crate does not want to

do my bidding. I must not be far from them. I have to follow. The light of the marker appears, and then disappears. It's not close. The wind is playing with it, and it's going to be difficult to climb on. The hard surface of the buoy will smash into anyone who tries to get close.

I am alone out here, hanging on to the mad crate. I cannot make out any movement from the two men. The marker is still far away. I am paddling, but the waves are against me.

The sea has betrayed me. I miscalculated. I should have trusted that sense of foreboding and the foul smell.

The darkness and the waves hide everything. Where is Abd al-Wahab?

If I paddled more furiously, I might reach him. I can't let him drown. But I'm starting to feel fatigued.

"God!" I shout, but the waves swallow my entreaty.

Where is Abd al-Wahab? I shout to him: "Abd al-Wahab!" I can sense him nearby. "Abd al-Wahab!"

I think I hear a voice, but it's the roar of the waves and the rain.

"Abd al-Wahab!" I strain to hear a response.

"Ali," I hear him reply. Abd al-Wahab is still alive. I look around me in all directions, but my eyes are blinded by the darkness.

"Abd al-Wahab!" I shout at the top of my voice.

"Yes." I'm like a ghost in the water, paddling, dragging the crate with me. I paddle on and on. Fatigue spreads through my arms, back and voice.

"I'll get you."

I make it over to Abd al-Wahab, dragging the crate with me. I can feel the exhaustion in my arms. Abd al-Wahab is close now.

"Give me your hand!" I grab his arm, and something trembles in my chest.

Chapter 7

11:00 p.m.

"The wind's changing direction," I tell Abd al-Wahab.

"We've moved away from the marker."

"I can't see its light. Maybe Sulayman made it."

"What with the waves, the sea and the wind . . ." I break off my sentence. I don't want to frighten him more. I feel his desperation.

"Let's just keep hanging onto the crate until the storm calms down."

The wind is blowing us further out to sea, but I don't tell Abd al-Wahab.

"I'm getting cold," he complains.

I try to keep his spirits up. "Keep going, my brother."

The wind and the rain increase the crate's wild movements.

How did you not take the storm into account, Ali? Its smell was hovering around your nose. You shouldn't have chanced it. How long will you go on being stubborn?

"How long has the storm been going on now?" Abd al-Wahab asks me.

"No idea."

"When the storm calms down, we might see a passing boat."

This idea cheers my soul. We go on shouting to each other in the dark.

"Sulayman has probably reached the marker," he says hopefully.

We've moved away from where the boat sank, and the light from the marker has disappeared.

When the storm passes, wherever I am, the direction of the shoreline will come to me. I am never wrong about where to find the coast and the isles of Kuwait.

Darkness brings confusion. I cannot see Abd al-Wahab. I reach out and feel his palm.

"We'll be saved."

Abd al-Wahab's strength gave out when the waves first started beating down on us. But I will keep a hold on him. I won't abandon him. We'll survive together or die together. Perhaps Sulayman has reached the marker and hauled himself out. If only Abd al-Wahab could reach it.

"Cold." His voice beseeches.

I can't help him. The water and the cold surround us on all sides. "The storm will calm down soon," I say. I hear no answer.

If anything happens to Abd al-Wahab, I will never be able to forgive myself.

"I'm going to tell you a story."

He's still quiet. I shout at him: "Abd al-Wahab!"

"Yes."

"I'm going to tell you about something that happened to me."

"I'm listening."

"We have to keep talking until the storm passes."

"When will it end?" His question wounds me. I wish I knew, my brother.

The sky is now hurling rain on us like sharp stones. We are two old men hanging on to a plastic crate.

Noura said "Don't go out today".

The cold and the rain are freezing my shoulders.

"What's the story?" Abd al-Wahab asks me.

"You know the one about when I fell into the sea, and how I was saved near the island of Salama in the Straits of Hormuz." I'll draw the story out to keep him alert.

"I was steering a merchant ship on her way back from a port in India, heading to Dubai. At midnight, I noticed the ship was listing. I yelled at the helmsman and rushed out of the wheelhouse. Are you listening, Abd al-Wahab?"

"I'm going to die."

"Don't think about death."

"I'm thinking about my kids." Abd al-Wahab's voice breaks the thing that's throbbing in my chest.

The storm is getting stronger. Who will be able to reach us in this darkness?

If the storm passes, I tell myself, I'll never put anyone's life at risk again!

"Abd al-Wahab." I shout into the darkness. "Please forgive me."

"Forgiven, my brother. This is what God Almighty has written."

"Don't give up. We're going to be saved." I yell at him, but it's as if I'm speaking to myself.

I'll tie one end the agal to Abd al-Wahab's arm and the other to the handle of the crate. Where's the agal? Where did it go? It's not around my neck. I've lost it without even noticing. The sea has taken it.

We've definitely moved further from the marker. No one will ever find Sulayman in this weather.

I have no idea whether the storm has affected our neighbourhood or not. If it has, my sons and my friends will have alerted the coastguard, and they'll be out here looking for us. At our last get-together with friends, we said that we'd be going out to the Aryaq fishing grounds, and Noura knows I'm out here.

"Finish your story."

Hearing Abd al-Wahab's voice gives me a glimmer of hope. I continue in a louder voice:

"The ship went down in conditions like these. The sailors put on their life jackets and threw themselves into the sea."

If only we had on our lifejackets. I don't know if

Abd al-Wahab can hear me.

"Abd al-Wahab!" I reach out, feeling for him.

"Why don't you answer me?"

"I don't know. I'm tired."

"Are you listening?"

"I'm cold. My teeth are chattering, and I'm dizzy."

"Keep a tight hold of the crate. Don't let it out of your hands. Stay near me."

"My whole body is shivering."

I have to distract him from his fear.

"Are you listening to me?"

"Yes."

"On the night the ship sank, the sailors managed to find a lifeboat, but one sailor had disappeared. We were out the whole night, struggling against the waves, shouting and looking for him. With morning light came hope. We were rescued by a ship, and I informed the captain that one of my sailors was missing . . . Are you listening, Abd al-Wahab?"

"I'm tired, and I'm going to die."

This scares me. "I feel the cold and exhaustion, too," I yell at him, "but we're going to be rescued."

I shouldn't have tried to resist the sea.

"Come closer to me."

The waves and wind are tossing the crate. Just find Abd al-Wahab's hand. I feel myself shivering and rebuke myself: Since when are you afraid, Ali!"

Why does your heart fail you? All your life you've

been saying, "The sea is my friend!"

I should have turned back to the shore the moment I woke up. I won't abandon Abd al-Wahab. Let me die and him live. The day the ship went down, I didn't abandon the lost sailor.

"Abd al-Wahab, can you hear me?" I stretch my arm out and grab his hand.

"Can you hear me?"

"I'm dizzy. Everything is spinning around me. And I'm tired. We've been at sea since noon. Water's getting in my ears!"

"Stay close to me."

Abd al-Wahab, don't leave me! Al-Najdi isn't afraid, only stay with him.

"Abd al-Wahab," I shout, but my voice comes out weakly. "I didn't abandon that sailor whom I didn't know. I stood up to the captain, and searched for the sailor until I found and rescued him. Are you listening to me?"

"Yes," he replies weakly.

"But I'm so tired," he complains.

"Hang on to the crate. Don't ever let go."

I open my eyes and try to focus on his face, but the darkness has blinded me.

You're too tired to be able to see any more, Najdi!

"Abd al-Wahab. Forgive me, my brother!" I yell.

"God is the Forgiver."

If I get through this, I'll never again take anyone to

sea with me.

Like Abd al-Wahab, I have started to get dizzy. The accursed waves are throwing me around, and the cold and rain are beating down on my head.

"I bear witness that there is no God but God." Abd al-Wahab's voice reaches me faintly through the darkness.

The voice of the ship's muezzin, Sultan, rings in my ears. He always called us to prayer on the dhow.

You've started shivering, Najdi, and your heart is weakening. You have a sharp pain in your back. Here you are in the storm, Najdi, in the rain and the cold, and you're so old. The cold feels like skewers in your neck and shoulder. You don't know, it might be two hours or more that you've been clutching the crate, your body swaying in the water.

Najdi, your friend the sea has turned against you. You've lived in its bosom since you were a child, and you never thought it would betray your friendship. You remember your wife Shamma once told you: "I'm afraid for you." You smiled at her and said: "Don't worry. I'm with my friend."

"The sea doesn't have friends." You remember her fear.

Shamma was worried about you, and even today Noura tried to warn you: "Stay at home."

Ever since you were small, you've only ever listened to the voice of your own soul. You have never been able to work for anyone. You have refused to be anything other than the master of your own soul. You insisted single-mindedly on becoming a shipmaster. You've never known any other work. You failed in all your attempts at doing business. All your life, you remained a mariner in search of adventure. Your friend the sea calls out to you, and you run to it.

The shipmasters in Kuwait call you the lion of the sea. They still talk of how you, with your courage and intelligence, beat a pirate and his gang just off Ras Shartibat. They attacked you by night. They surrounded you in an attempt to steal the dhow's cargo and everything else on board. You pretended to give in to their demands and then calmly leaned over your tool box, as if looking for the clasp, and then brandished your revolver in their faces and screamed like a man possessed: "I'll get you for this, you dogs!"

They threw their rifles down and jumped overboard to save themselves. You knew your revolver wasn't loaded, but you took a risk, and you had the strength and dignity to stand up to them.

So how can a lion be afraid? How can a lion of the sea dread the sea?

You've been a friend of the sea since childhood, but the storm has betrayed you.

All my life, whenever fate placed me a tricky situation, I have prayed to God, and He has sent help. Will

I drown just off the coast of Kuwait? How can a valiant captain, who has battled the high seas, drown in a passing storm just off the shore from his home?

O sea, I left the world behind for your sake. How can you betray me?

I am shipmaster Ali, son of Nasser al-Najdi. I have known the terrors of the world's seas and ventured into the ocean's night, and now I'm drowning just off the shore from my home!

I once told Abdallah al-Qutami: "My end will be in the sea."

But I didn't mean in the sea of Kuwait, my own country! A passing squall taking Ali al-Najdi!

What use will that be to you, Oh sea?

I have started to shiver. My fingers can hardly hold onto the crate. Perhaps Sulayman has made it onto the marker. Someone or other will save him, and then they'll come for us. No, I won't give up, and I won't abandon my friend.

"Abd al-Wahab," I shout.

"Where are you, Abd al-Wahab?"

Abd al-Wahab is nowhere near me. The edges of the crate are all empty. Abd al-Wahab's hand has disappeared from the crate. Abd al-Wahab has drowned.

"Oh God," I shout in terror. "Abd al-Wahab!"

The rain and waves ignore my cries, and the sea along with them.

There is no one near me. I am all alone, clinging to

the crate.

Abd al-Wahab. Please don't drown. Abd al-Wahab, please be swimming somewhere.

I can't see a thing. It's all darkness, and waves and rain.

My friend has drowned, and I . . . I'm as tired as you, Abd al-Wahab.

I should have kept hold of your arm. You told me you felt dizzy, and you told your brother Sulayman that you were going to die.

I'm all alone in the nothingness of the sea. The sea has betrayed me, using the storm.

I should have gone back to shore. The smell I sensed was a premonition, but . . .

The accursed rain is pounding down on my head, making me so dizzy I might drown. My hips ache.

I haven't heard a sound from Abd al-Wahab. I can't hear him calling for help. He was next to me, clinging on to the crate.

I hold on to the crate as it fills up with water. I will not give up. I'm going to keep hold of the crate.

The headband is lost. The sea has stolen it.

The storm will pass, and I will survive.

Chapter 8

11:30 p.m.

Two boys have grabbed hold of me. They have pushed my legs violently against the bastinado rope restraints, and the mullah beats them with his stick. "No! No!" I scream, but no sound emerges. The mullah is beating me. I want to resist. I will put up a fight, and I will not agree to his demands. I'll scream right at him: "I will be a shipmaster."

Where am I? I'm surrounded by water and waves. Perhaps a fleeting sleep stole over me. My hip aches.

Where did this dream come from? My fingers are still holding onto the edge of the crate. How much time has passed? I feel numb from the cold, and the rain feels as though it's splitting open my head.

I didn't expect a storm today. Nor did I expect the sea to be like this.

I am a son of the sea, so why should the sea break its son's back? Why would the sea deny me after all our decades together?

What harm could it do the sea to have a captain as a friend?

I'm alone in the darkness. It's cold, and I feel dizzy. Even if a ship were to pass now, no one would notice me. However, I will not let myself be hidden. I'll scream and shout. I have no idea what time it is. If the storm would stop, I'd be able to make out the coast, as the Kuwaiti shoreline is engraved upon my heart.

The boat has gone down, Sulayman has swum over to the marker, and Abd al-Wahab – I don't know how he could have abandoned me.

My head is uncovered. The waves will rock me to sleep, but I will not sleep. I'll stay awake until the storm passes. Then I will rebuke the sea.

If I had my agal, I'd be able to attach myself to the handle of the crate.

I've been through so many storms at sea. Along with my men – my sailors – we managed to deal with the storms. We kept the dhow stable. Everyone stuck to his spot, and we all stayed alert, calling on God for help: "Oh Lord!"

Tonight, the sea has betrayed me. I'm your friend, Sea.

My mother said: "The sea has no friends!"

"No, it was I who told you that, my son."

"Father? How have you come to the crate?"

"I told you, the sea is treacherous."

"The sea sent a signal. I smelled its scent, Father. It passed by my nose, but . . ." I was a small boy walking on the surface of the sea until I reached heaven.

What's this? I'm on my own here.

It's cold. Abd al-Wahab's teeth were chattering, and he'd grown dizzy before he drowned. I will keep hold of the crate. If I let go, I'll float on my back. Abd al-Wahab hasn't drowned. He has swum to his brother Sulayman. I'm sure his brother rescued him.

I remembered the accident, when my brother Abdallah carried the child onto the lifeboat. The woman screamed to me: "You saved my boy!"

Salem's wife, the young Indian woman, was beautiful. I gave him money so he would stay with her.

"You used to give me money each time you went off to sea."

"Shamma! What's come over you? The rain will soak your clothes. By God, Shamma, I haven't forgotten you. I told you: you're a captain . . ."

I'm alone. My teeth are chattering.

What does the sea gain from passing this judgment?

Why does the storm continue to shake me? I can't do anything more. I'm tired. I'm an old man drifting in the sea with nothing to cover my body but my long underwear.

That's enough now, Sea. I know the storm will pass, so why do you drag this out? I don't think you want me to die. Maybe you missed me and wanted me to stay with you a little longer.

If a wave washes me ashore, how will I face people?

Some unlucky woman must have slipped past the guards and walked along the boom, bringing her bad luck to me.

"I told you." I can hear the voice of Shamma, my wife. It's dark. I feel as if Shamma is clutching the crate in front of me.

"Shamma? How are you drowning with us?"

"I told you I was worried about you."

I'm so cold, Shamma. The rain is lashing my head, and I have shooting pains in my hips.

Shamma? Where have you gone?

I look around, but the darkness has stopped up my eyes. The waves jerk me around, and it's cold.

"Are you going to die in the sea?"

"No, I'm not going to die."

"You'll die."

I know that voice. It's my dear friend Muhammad al-Qutami.

"Muhammad died in the market when police shot him. I'm Abdallah al-Qutami."

"Abdallah? How did you know where I'd be? Where's your boat? Where's the dhow? We were sailing along beside each other, and now you've come to save me. Hold on to the edge of the crate until your ship arrives."

"You'll die at sea. You told me."

"No, I'm not going to die. A shipmaster doesn't die. I'm staying alive at sea."

"You won't abandon me . . . Abdallah. Where are you?"

"How come you've been shipwrecked, Captain?"

"The wind plotted against me and kindled the sea's fury."

"That's not Abdallah's voice!"

"I'm Alan Villiers."

"The Australian, the Englishman. Come on, keep hold of the crate. You are a sea captain and you must have a lifeboat here with you. You and I will go back to Kuwait together. This time, you must stay in my house in Kayfan. I won't let you stay in anyone else's house."

"I told you not to steer your ship without lights."

"The storm smashed the boat's lantern."

"You're a brave man, Najdi! I've seen you in all sorts of conditions."

"But it was you who said Arab sailors don't like the deep sea and that they cling to the coastline."

"I was wrong."

"I knew you were watching me."

"I've seen how skilled and brave you are. Why aren't you wearing a lifejacket, Najdi?"

"They were getting in our way, and the boat went down before we could put them on. Have you brought your book with you?"

"My book is always with me."

"Are there pictures in it? Where's the lifeboat – the

one that's going to rescue us? Alan, where have you gone?"

"And how can a captain let a sailor drown?"

I'm not a sailor. I'm a shipmaster. I am Ali. God has blessed me with five boys: Husayn, Abd al-Wahab, Uthman, Sulayman and Khalid. Shamma gave birth to my youngest, Khaled, while I was out at sea. I left her pregnant and, when I returned, she had Khaled on her lap. I'm sure my boys will be looking for me. They'll come save me, and so will the coastguard . . .

"Shamma. The rain is drenching you. You'll drown with me."

"I'm not going to drown."

"I'll hold your hand."

I'm alone, holding onto the crate. If the rain were to stop, if the cold were to stop . . . My head is buzzing. I can no longer open my eyes.

When I was young, I would swim the whole day and fear would swim along with me.

Now I'm over seventy.

Why would the sea kill an old sailor?

God, why?

My children and grandchildren are back there in my house in Kayfan, and I'm out here alone in the darkness.

Where am I? The ill-starred storm has not come to an end, and I'm out here with a fish crate.

The cassette recorder has sunk, and along with it the

voices of Awad al-Dokhy and Shadi al-Khaleej.

My sister Maryam has come over to ask me: "Have mercy on Shamma."

"My brother, apple of my eye."

"Maryam, you shouldn't have come. I'm almost naked, Maryam. I don't want any of my sailors to see you. Hold on tight to the crate. Maryam, have you brought a lantern with you? You were always cleaning the lanterns. Maryam, why are you crying? Don't cry, Maryam, your brother's not going to die."

"My boy," the woman shouted.

"I saved your boy, so why are you shouting?"

I knew there were sharks all around. With all that scrambling about, the passengers could have over-turned the ship, but my brother Abdallah and the singer Ismail saved your boy . . . But how is it that you, a woman of no relation, have come out here?"

"I'm Latifa, your sister."

"Latifa . . . I'm hungry. My hips are hurting. The bread is going to get soaked. But it might warm my hand."

The black waves are now turning red. That's the blood of the sea, the blood that taints me.

I cannot keep holding onto the crate.

It's a squid squirting red blood, but the darkness . . .

I am not a small child who can't swim.

My father used to watch me when al-Qutami and I were in our boat. My mother forbade him to come out with me. The Kuwaiti captains trade in pearls, and I chose the sea. I chose to become a sea-faring captain. I hated to work on shore. I hate humiliation.

I will get through this storm. I will make my kufiyah into a sail and attach it to the crate.

We will sail until we reach the shore. I won't lose my way. Where is my kufiyah?

"My brother, apple of my eye."

"Don't worry, Maryam. Why are you crying?"

O God, I'm so tired. The stones of rain pound against my head. I can hear nothing. The cold is tearing through my flesh.

I am all alone. I cannot catch my breath. I have been calling the sea my friend for years.

How will I return to Kuwait? My brothers urged me to sell my ship, the *Bayan*.

"You'll bring wood back from India."

"I'm so tired, Father. I've been hanging onto the crate for an hour, for two hours, for three . . . I'm so tired. I've been hanging on to it since yesterday or the day before.

I've been holding onto the dhow my whole life, Father. My whole life. That night, I stood in front of the boom. It was looking at me reproachfully. I heard the sails weep.

Now the storm and the waves are playing with me. In the darkness, I see nothing.

I don't know what has happened to Sulayman. Perhaps he reached the marker. And as for Abd al-Wahab
. . .

The storm sunk the boat and it took Abd al-Wahab.

I don't know where I have ended up. The waves have tossed me around so much — not to mention the rain, the cold, the darkness and the blood.

My body is sticky and bloodstained.

"Ali."

In the darkness, it's as if my father is coming. The boat has sunk, Father. Why didn't you bring the lantern? Take me and my brother Ibrahim home. I was sleeping and was washed out to sea, Father. I was just having a nap after lunch. I promise I will never sleep on the sea shore again.

Which way is the coast? The position of the coast is engraved in my mind, but there is no coast anywhere near.

My head will explode from the beating of the rain.

I am going to let go of the crate and start swimming. I won't keep holding on to the fish crate.

I'll swim, and perhaps I'll come across the dhow of Captain Yusuf al-Qutami. He'll come and take me. I'll reach the shore.

Noura asked me: "What time will you be home?" I won't be late. I wasn't expecting a storm.

The waves will carry me.

I remember that, ever since I was a child, I could lie

on my back with my arms spread and let the sea take me with it.

Ah. It's cold. I can't see ... The sky has placed a blanket of darkness over my face.

The crate has become heavy. I'm not going to keep clinging to it. I'll let go. The fish will get away – those big sobaity.

My friend the sea will carry me home. Shamma and the children, and my nephews and nieces, are waiting for me.

I am Captain Ali al-Najdi. I will not surrender, and no one will twist my arm.

I'll swim. The storm will pass, and either I'll find the shore or it will find me.

I can hear the voice of Sultan, the dhow's muezzin. My brother Abdallah is on the dhow, along with Hamed bin Salem al-Omar. They must have come to rescue me.

I will not humiliate myself. I will not ride with a stranger.

I can hear the sound of the ship cutting its way through the water. I raised the mainsail during the night. I was steering my ship through the terrors.

Alan used to be afraid of the dark. I am not afraid.

I hear the voice of Sultan, the muezzin. I will repeat after him:

"I bear witness that there is no god but God."

I feel light now. I've let go of the crate. I'm swimming on my back. Nothing is weighing me down. I feel light.

The water comes at me from all sides.

Why, Sea? Al-Najdi is your son, so why . . . I feel sure that you want me for yourself, so that we'll stay together.

I'm your son, Sea. I'm a part of you. I'm a sea captain.

The ship will come to me. My beloved dhow, the *Bayan*.

I'll stay in the sea until it arrives.

I shall not leave the sea.

Kuwait, 12 December 2016

ABOUT THE AUTHOR

Taleb Alrefai was born in Kuwait in 1958 and started
writing short stories as an engineering student at the
University of Kuwait in the mid–1970s, publishing in
local newspapers. His first collection, *Tal 'Umrak Abu
'Ujjaj* (Live Long Abu 'Ujjaj) was published in 1992.
Between 2003 and 2008 he worked for Kuwait's
National Council for Culture, Art, and Literature, and
edited their monthly arts review, *Jaridat Al Funoon*. He
published six more collections of short stories before
writing his first novel *Dhil al-Shams* (2000, Shadow of
the Sun), centred on migrant Egyptian workers in

146

Kuwait. In 2002, he won the State Prize for Letters for his novel, *Ra'ihat al-Bahr* (Scent of the Sea). His novel *Fi al-Huna* (Here and There) was longlisted for the 2016 International Prize for Arabic Fiction and has been published in French translation. In 2011 he founded Al-Multaqa (Cultural Circle), a regular literary discussion forum in Kuwait City, which led to the founding of the annual Almultaqa Prize for the Arabic Short Story in 2016. His novel *Al-Najdi* (2017, *The Mariner*) also has a French edition. He lives in Kuwait City.

ABOUT THE TRANSLATOR

Russell Harris holds an MA in Oriental Studies from Balliol College, Oxford, and is an established translator of literary works from French and Arabic. He is a contributor to the *Dictionary of National Biography, The Routledge Encyclopedia of 19th Century Photography, The Oxford Companion to Food* and *The Encyclopaedia Islamica*. He has written many articles on Middle Eastern art for various international journals and magazines. His translations include works by Naguib Mahfouz, Alaa al-Aswany and Tawfiq al-Hakim. He currently works as an editor at The Institute of Ismaili Studies, London.

OTHER TITLES FROM BANIPAL BOOKS

Mansi: A Rare Man in His Own Way by Tayeb Salih
ISBN 978-0-9956369-8-9 • Paperback • 184pp • 2020
Translated and introduced by Adil Babikir, this affectionate
memoir of Salih's irrepressible friend Mansi shows, with humour,
wit, and 20th century personalities centre stage, another side to
the Sudanese author, internationally renowned for his classic
novel *Season of Migration to the North*

Goat Mountain by Habib Selmi
ISBN: 978-1-913043-04-9 • Paperback • 98pp • 2020
Translated from the Arabic by Charis Olszok. The author's debut
novel, from 1988, now in English translation. The journey to
Goat Mountain, a forlorn, dusty, desert Tunisian village, begins in
a dilapidated old bus. "I enjoyed this book. I liked its gloomy
atmosphere, its strangeness and sense of unfamiliarity. Eerie,
funereal, and outstanding!" – Jabra Ibrahim Jabra

A Boat to Lesbos, and other poems by Nouri Al-Jarrah
ISBN: 978-0-9956369-4-1 • Paperback • 120pp • 2018
Translated from the Arabic by Camilo Gómez-Rivas and Allison
Blecker and illustrated with paintings by Reem Yassouf. The first
English-language collection for this major Syrian poet, whose
compelling epic poem bears passionate witness to Syrian families
fleeing to Lesbos through the eye of history, of Sappho and the
travels of Odysseus.

An Iraqi In Paris by Samuel Shimon
ISBN: 978-0-9574424-8-1 • Paperback • 282pp • 2016
Translated from the Arabic by Christina Philips and Piers
Amodia with the author. Long-listed for the 2007 IMPAC Prize.
Called a gem of autobiographical writing, a manifesto of
tolerance, a cinematographic odyssey. "This combination of a
realist style with content more akin to the adventures of Sindbad
helps to make *An Iraqi in Paris* a modern Arab fable, sustaining
the moral such a fable requires: follow your dreams and you will
succeed" – Hanna Ziadeh, *Al-Ahram Weekly*

Heavenly Life: Selected Poems by Ramsey Nasr
ISBN: 978-0-9549666-9-0 • Paperback • 180pp • 2010
The first English-language collection for Ramsey Nasr, Poet
Laureate of the Netherlands, 2009 & 2010. Translated from the
Dutch by David Colmer, with an Introduction by Victor
Schiferli and a Foreword by Ruth Padel. The title poem was
written to commemorate the 150th anniversary of Gustav
Mahler's birth and is based on his Fourth Symphony, the four
sections of the poem echoing the structure, tone and length of
its movements. It is named after "Das himmlische Leben", the
song that forms the symphony's finale.

Knife Sharpener: Selected Poems by Sargon Boulus
ISBN: 978-0-9549666-7-6 • Paperback • 154pp • 2009
The first English-language collection for this influential and
innovative Iraqi poet, who dedicated himself to reading, writing
and translating into Arabic contemporary poetry. Foreword by
Adonis. Translated from the Arabic by the author with an essay
"Poetry and Memory". Includes tributes by fellow poets and
authors following the author's passing while the book was in
production, and an Afterword by the publisher.

Shepherd of Solitude: Selected Poems by Amjad Nasser
ISBN: 978-0-9549666-8-3 • Paperback • 186pp • 2009
The first English-language collection for this major modern
poet, who lived most of his life outside his home country of
Jordan. Translated from the Arabic and introduced by the
foremost translator of contemporary Arabic poetry into English,
Khaled Mattawa, with the poems selected by poet and translator
from the poet's Arabic volumes from the years 1979 to 2004.

**Mordechai's Moustache and his Wife's Cats, and other
stories** by Mahmoud Shukair
ISBN: 978-0-9549666-3-8 • Paperback • 124 pages • 2007
Translations from the Arabic by Issa J Boullata, Elizabeth
Whitehouse, Elizabeth Winslow and Christina Phillips. This first
major publication in an English translation of one of the most
original of Palestinian storytellers enthralls, surprises and even
shocks. "Shukair's gift for absurdist satire is never more telling
than in the hilarious title story" – Judith Kazantsis

A Retired Gentleman, and other stories by Issa J Boullata.
ISBN: 978-0-9549666-6-9 • Paperback • 120 pages • 2007
The Jerusalem-born author, scholar, critic, and translator creates a
rich medley of tales by emigrants to Canada and the US from
Palestine, Lebanon, Egypt and Syria. George, Kamal, Mayy,
Abdullah, Nadia, William all have to begin their lives again, learn
how to deal with their memories, with their pasts . . .

The Myrtle Tree by Jad El Hage.
ISBN: 978-0-9549666-4-5 • Paperback • 288 pages • 2007
"This remarkable novel, set in a Lebanese mountain village,
conveys with razor-sharp accuracy the sights, sounds, tastes and
tragic dilemmas of Lebanon's fratricidal civil war. A must read" –
Patrick Seale

Unbuttoning the Violin
Poems & short stories from Banipal Live 2006
ISBN: 0-9549666-2-7 • Paperback • 128pp • 2006
Selected works by poets Joumana Haddad from Lebanon and
Abed Ismael from Syri, and fiction writers Mansoura Ez-Eldin
from Egypt and Ala Hlehel from Palestine. The 2006 Banipal
Live UK tour was a partnership of Banipal magazine with the
British Council and The Reading Agency.

Sardines and Oranges: Short Stories from North Africa
ISBN: 978-0-9549666-1-4 • Paperback • 222 pages • 2005
Introduced by Peter Clark. The 26 stories are by 21 authors:
Latifa Baqa, Ahmed Bouzfour, Rachida el-Charni, Mohamed
Choukri, Mohammed Dib, Tarek Eltayeb, Mansoura Ez-Eldin,
Gamal el-Ghitani, Said al-Kafrawi, Idriss el-Kouri, Ahmed el-
Madini, Ali Mosbah, Hassouna Mosbahi, Sabri Moussa,
Muhammad Mustagab, Hassan Nasr, Rabia Raihane, Tayeb Salih,
Habib Selmi, Izz al-Din Tazi and Mohammed Zefzaf.
Translations are from the Arabic except for Mohammed Dib's
story, which was from French.